The Essential Immigrant

The Essential Immigrant

Dan Lacey

HIPPOCRENE BOOKS
New York

For information address
Hippocrene Books
171 Madison Ave.
New York, NY 10016

Library of Congress Cataloging-in-Publication Data

Lacey, Dan.
  The essential immigrant / Dan Lacey
    p.   cm.
  ISBN 0-87052-610-3
  1. United States—Emigration and immigration—Govern-
ment policy. 2. United—Emigration and immigration. 3.
Immigrants—United States. I. Title.
JV6483.L33   1990
325.73—dc20   89-29722
                                                          CIP

Editorial development, design and production by
Combined Books, Inc., 26 Summit Grove Ave., Suite 207,
Bryn Mawr, PA 19010, (215) 527-9276.

Printed in the United States.

Acknowledgments

Many people assisted and encouraged me in the creation of this book.

My wife, Margaret, continued her unwavering support of my work despite the demands of her own blossoming career. I shall always be humbled by her unselfishness, determination and endurance.

Jon Gordon, whose professional competence and empathy for photojournalistic subjects are unprecedented in my experience, kept me informed of West Coast immigration developments during times when I was elsewhere.

Lourdes Regala, who has walked many unconventional paths with me, sacrificed the thrill of watching her own prime-time television acting debut on *Dallas* so that she could help us get to know the poor-but-friendly people of Tijuana's Murua.

Suzanne and Peter Flynn generously supported me and my team with friendship, food and luxurious housing, as well as giving us entre to the story-book social life of California's Laguna Beach.

Dr. Anita Figueredo, an active supporter and personal friend of Mother Teresa, provided us with an introduction to the Reverend Joseph Langford and his band of missionaries—and with the map we very much needed to find the order's headquarters in Mexico.

Christine Semenza assisted me in researching the role that her great-grandfather, the late Senator Patrick A. McCarran, played in the formulation of American immigration policy. Susan E. Searcy, manuscript curator for the library of the University of Nevada-Reno, assisted me energetically in those matters, as well.

Robert L. Brown, a district director for the U.S. Immigration and Naturalization Service was—contrary to the prevailing image of that agency—friendly, open and extremely helpful.

And, as usual, George Blagowidow and Jacek Galazka of Hippocrene Books served as the world-wise intellectual sounding boards that every journalist craves but few are ever fortunate enough to find.

To these and all the other people who helped in their own special ways, I offer my heart-felt thanks.

To Florence and Harold, with gratitude.

Contents

Introduction

I N AMERICAN JOURNALISM SCHOOLS they teach a three-part formula for effective editorial opinion writing: first, make a contention; second, substantiate that contention with facts and statistics; finally, and most importantly, suggest a constructive solution to the problem.

Usually the formula is easy to follow and works very well. Indeed, when you read a "Letter to the Editor" that is particularly striking, you'd be likely to find that it was written by someone who is in on this little trade secret. But when *The New York Times* editorial writers attempted in 1989 to deal with the question of whether or not America needs to prepare for a shortage of citizens in the 21st century, they stumbled on that essential third component.

In a lead editorial entitled "The Right Number of Americans," they made the contention that a number of people were sounding too urgent an alarm over the looming population shortage. To substantiate that contention, they cited a number of statistics from such sources as the Census Bureau that show that the quantitative changes in U.S. population are taking place much more gradually than the persons sounding the alarms imply.

The editorial writers had set the stage for a powerful suggestion of how America could deal constructively with concerns about population in a calm, long-term way, yet they failed to utilize the opportunity. Instead, they choked up and concluded merely that: "The right number of Americans is the number we can live with."

Is that a constructive solution, as required by the formula for good editorial writing? Although I've pondered it at length, I still can't figure out what it means. What did they mean by the number "we can live with"? How can we know how many people "we can live with," and how can each of us participate in setting that standard? That editorial certainly raised more questions than it answered, but such is the nature of most of what is written about American immigration issues.

To a large extent my attention has been called to the subject of America's attitudes toward immigrants by the reaction I've received to a chapter in my previous book, *The Paycheck Disruption*, entitled "The Riddle of the Wretched Refuse." In that chapter I discussed the fact that mass immigration had been essential to the growth of the U.S. economy to world leadership. A surprising number of people have since told me that, prior to reading that chapter, they had never known or thought about the connection between immigration and America's economic success in this century.

As a writer I feel good that I've been able to educate, but as an American citizen I'm more than a bit ashamed that we haven't made this information an essential part of our educational process.

On a more emotional level, I've been driven to write this book by a sort of double vision that I've developed in the course of my research, speaking and writing on employment-related subjects throughout the United States.

There are few cities in America of the late 20th century where one does not encounter people whose outward appearance clashes with the northwest European ethnic standard that we have come to regard as a true American look—the look that still dominates most of our mass communications media and which some observers have dubbed "Eurocentricity." The diversity of cultures is particularly evident in Los Angeles, where I have spent about one third of my time in recent years. I admit that, as with most Americans of European descent, my first glimpse of people from non-European countries sometimes generates gut emotions of annoyance, resentment or fear.

But then these people change, right before my eyes, into clones of my own immigrant grandparents and those of many of the people I know and love. My fears and other anxieties turn to admiration mixed with a benign form of envy: Their wondrous adventure of moving to America, long the center of mankind's attention, from a place of much less opportunity is one that I will never experience.

My double-vision in regard to opportunity-seeking immigrants also can be attributed in part to the fact that until about the age of seven I shared my room with an uncle who—despite the fact that he had been born in America and fought in the American forces in Europe for most of World War II and worked hard after returning from the war—lacked the resources to set up a home of his own. He and my mother were American-born children of European immigrants to America who, like hundreds of thousands of others, had been kept in poverty by the corrupt and exploitive practices of Pennsylvania's anthracite coal mining industry.

My uncle and I were a strange set of roommates. I was

a little boy who had never even seen the other side of town, and he was a young man who had had to sleep next to corpses on the beaches of Normandy. I was at the stage where photos of Roy Rogers and his horse Trigger were my favorite decor item, while my uncle's tastes ran to backlighted Blue Ribbon beer signs.

Nevertheless, we were buddies. He took me for haircuts and on excursions downtown. By sharing my room with him until he could go out and establish a home and family of his own, I learned how to play polkas and World War II battlefield favorites on the harmonica— and the indelible lesson that people who start off with their nose in the mud are the ones most determined to rise above it. All they really require is the opportunity to do so.

My uncle is retired now, owns a very nice home, drives a late-model car, and he and his wife have a son who is a successful computer systems analyst and has a home of his own. So when I'm having a big-time day and I'm dressed in a Brooks Brothers custom-made suit and dining in Manhattan or Beverly Hills, I have to scoff to myself when people complain about the way the Puerto Ricans, Koreans, blacks, Vietnamese, Nicaraguans, Mexicans, Filipinos or whoever on the other side of town are junking up the area by living three generations to a house. Little more than three decades ago some people must have said the same kind of things when Uncle Bill and I walked down the street.

Millions of other American families can tell similar stories, and encountering some of their anecdotes in the newspaper and magazine stacks of libraries has been one of the most rewarding and encouraging aspects of my research for this book.

Buried in one newspaper story on Chinese-Americans I found an anecdote about a New York City family in which the parents came to the United States in the early '60s. The father never learned English, and he worked six days a week, 12 hours a day, as a cook with no employment benefits. The mother also worked six days a week, 11 hours a day, in a garment factory. Their three children had, however, done much better. Their daughter earned a bachelor's degree and holds a corporate executive position. One son is a stockbroker, and the other is a lawyer. While the children were growing up, the story pointed out, the entire family had shared one bedroom. Compared to them, I realized while reading that story, mine had been a childhood of privilege.

In researching America's contemporary attitudes toward immigrants, I've encountered a very serious problem with America's mainstream, corporate-owned news media—an industry of which I was once an employee, but which I left behind in the early 1980s for the sake of professional freedom. To most of them, I've found, the story of America's contemporary immigration controversies is a police story, primarily a question of how to keep "them" on the other side of the fence, ditch or ocean. The idea that America needs to keep out newcomers, it seems, has become the standard wisdom, a given.

In the summer of 1988, for example, I talked with a reporter for the Los Angeles Times who had written extensively about the U.S. government's efforts to keep Mexicans from entering America illegally. I wanted to obtain some insight (and some street directions) from him before venturing into the Mexican side of the immigration story, and he was more than generous with his time. But try as I might to explain to him that I was writing about the human aspects of economics, not police activity, he insisted that what I was writing was just a "bromide," that everyone already knew about all the trouble down there.

However, in hundreds of subsequent conversations on the subject, I have never encountered one person who was previously aware of the fact that the Missionaries of Charity Fathers had established their world headquarters just a few miles south of the Tijuana/San Diego border to deal with the misery that America's anti-immigration policies and activities have created there.

A few months after my conversation with the man at the *Los Angeles Times*, a friend who is the business editor of a major daily newspaper in the East told me he couldn't accept the premise of this book for a completely different reason. "How can we maintain our competitive edge in manufacturing if we don't ship the work to Third World countries?" he argued. I tried to convince him that, in the context of America's overriding concern about the creation and preservation of jobs within America, his logic was akin to that of having someone eat your food for you. He couldn't agree with that, so we rescued our friendship by agreeing that the subject was so broad and complex that it would require an entire book to explore.

Conversely, many people outside the news media who I thought would have no interest in the subject of immigration have reacted with excitement upon hearing about this book. On airplanes, at dinner parties and at family gatherings I've found much unexpected encouragement in the number of questions people have asked me on this subject. From New York to Miami, to San Diego, to San Francisco, people outside the mainstream news media have cheered me on. Americans cherish their tradition as a nation of immigrants, but they know little about that tradition other than their own family experiences—and most seem to want to know much more.

Particularly ardent in their enthusiasm have been some of my friends who are natives (or the local equivalent thereof) of Southern California. While admitting that they don't understand the economic and political issues involved, they have learned pragmatically since childhood the self-interested wisdom of letting a highly motivated, economically less-fortunate immigrant do their heavy lifting while that immigrant is enroute to better opportunities.

One of my most profound challenges in writing this book has been that of trying to divorce myself from my own ethnic and racial identity, to put myself in the mindset of a third party who is neither a native-born American nor someone seeking to become an American.

Several years ago Lynne Chiara, former editor of *Personnel Administrator* magazine and my co-editor on *Work in the 21st Century*, sensitized me to the differences in male and female writing. Now that I've mastered gender-free writing to a point, I'm working on developing a point of view that is also free of ethnic and racial inhibitions and assumptions. Although I'm sure I slipped back into my white, male, American self at more than just a few points in the telling of this story, I hope I've accomplished my goal sufficiently to make this book of value to people of all backgrounds and situations.

I hope also that I've succeeded in exploring this subject in a way that will sensitize other American journalists to the human side of the immigration controversy that transcends contemporary American romanticism. More than anything, I hope they come to see the booming *maquiladoras* along America's south-west border as something other than a wonderful industrial development trend. History will, I am sure, remember those who promote and encourage such installations with disdain. As Ralph Waldo Emerson once pointed out: "If you put a chain around the neck of a slave, the other end fastens itself around your own."

There is also a strong element of self-interest for me in this work: My life has been filled with hybridized sensory wonders that exist only because the America of earlier times opened its arms to the most troubled and impoverished people of the world and said, "Please come in."

From one side of America to the other I've enjoyed an ever-changing flow of the mixed-up music, foods, art, philosophies, laughter, passions and pursuits of dozens of America's diverse cultures, and I would miss it all badly if America ever succeeded, as Adolph Hitler once thought it might, in institutionalizing an "American" race.

I also hope, therefore, that I have succeeded in exploring the story of America's evolving attitude toward immigrants in such a way that many of those who read this book will realize they, too, owe a large debt to the diversity born of mass immigration. Armed with this information, common Americans may be able to bring about immigration attitudes and policies which will break the cycle of fear and resentment that has never really benefitted anyone but some exploitive politicians and the pettiest, most paranoid members of their constituencies.

Indeed, I hope that I have helped to usher in a time when the term "FOB" or "Fresh Off the Boat," used derisively for decades on newcomers to America, will be a great compliment. There are no inferior peoples, only inferior motives and intentions. To date, not one wave of immigrants to America has demonstrated that their motives for making the move, or their intentions for the future of their adopted home, were anything less than the highest. Perhaps, some day, the Land of Immigrants' attitudes toward immigrants will acknowledge that.

Dan Lacey
Sandusky Bay, Ohio
July 1989

CHAPTER 1

A Country of Immigrants Where Values Collide

S MILES SHOULD NOT COME EASILY in this place called "Murua." Terraced haphazardly into the hills behind Tijuana's frenetic bus depot, it is a neighborhood that comprises some of the worst tangible evidence of Mexico's corruption-gutted economy—and the destitution that befalls those unwilling or unable to make a deal with the ruling powers.

As photographer Jon Gordon and I wander into Murua's dusty unpaved streets to research a magazine article, we see one family after another huddled into small spaces of relative privacy created by the architecture of poverty. The families gather in tiny courtyards delineated by rusty barbed wire and corrugated steel, and in minuscule rooms usually formed—walls and roof—from panels of laminated cardboard and delaminating plywood.

The entrances to many of these meager residences are secured by ornate doors long retired from much more elaborate structures. The exterior walls of many of Murua's homes are decorated with brightly colored panels of wood, plastic and metal rescued from building demolition sites. If the suffering that it connotes could be overlooked, this hodgepodge of shapes, colors and textures might be revered as a form of folk art.

But the suffering cannot be overlooked. The very smell of it touches our faces as we walk past the dented, uncovered metal drums that hold each family's supply of water for washing and cleaning. The suffering echoes in the weak barks of the bony stray dogs that lie in Murua's streets. We see it in the eyes of shoeless children who follow us through the streets, hounding us for pocket change. And as night falls, poverty fully exposes its dark face: in Murua, merely having a light in your hovel is utter luxury.

Yet the people smile broadly at us as we walk past. Much of their friendliness is merely a cultural tradition, of course. But they are also smiling because, despite their sad situations, we two light-skinned, comfortably dressed men who parked their brand new car at the edge of the neighborhood are living symbols of *El Norte*, The North—the United States of America, the place of economic freedom to which the citizens of Murua dream of going to build a better life.

Seeing us in their streets reassures them that they are nearer than ever to their dreams. They grin, wave, and even thank us for taking their photographs. They seem not to know that as a society Americans are determined, perhaps more than ever before in history, to prevent impoverished people of other lands from becoming U.S. citizens.

Needed But Unwanted

That such poverty exists on earth is no surprise, of course. Virtually every American has read about, or even seen on television, the material sparseness of such faraway places as Bangladesh. But to confront such misery face-to-face among hard-working families who reside less than 10 miles outside the United States and less than a 20-minute drive from San Diego, one of America's most affluent communities, is—to say the very least—embarrassing.

Our discomfort was made worse by the knowledge that these people were actually quite valuable to the American economy. Indeed, some of the most aggressive industrial development projects in the United States were being built just a few miles from Murua's small streets with the expressed purpose of utilizing the labor of such impoverished Mexicans.

On our way to Murua, Jon and I had passed luxurious rows of newly planted palm trees lining the entrances to several large business parks along the American side of the border in a flatlands area known as "Otey Mesa." However, the splendor of the surroundings belies the fact that those parks were being developed on what has become known euphemistically in America's business circles as the "twin-factory" principle: a building primarily for white-collar workers on the American side of the border, with a "twin" factory for Mexican sweat labor on the other side.

There are more than 1,300 such factories on Mexico's side of the nearly 2,000 miles of border that it shares with the United States. More than 90 percent of them are owned by U.S. corporations, and most of the rest are owned by Japanese companies. In the jargon of the border, these factories have become known as *maquiladoras*, roughly the Spanish equivalent of "mill."

Like farmers of earlier times who brought their grains to a miller to be made into flour, manufacturers from America and other countries bring unfinished goods to the *maquiladoras* so that plentiful and cheap Mexican labor can convert them into saleable products that can then be shipped out to affluent countries. The Mexican and American governments have legislated free-trade zones, without the customary import and export tariffs, to accommodate the new factories. More than 400,000 Mexicans, drawn primarily from Murua and similar neighborhoods, were workng in the *maquiladoras* in 1989 for wages as low as 30 cents per hour and averaging, by most accounts, about $1 per hour.

The level of business growth within the *maquiladora* developments is so great—in 1989, new plants were opening within them at a rate of about 11 per month—that America's largest accounting practices and several law firms have opened branch offices along the U.S.-Mexico border to support the growing hoard of corporate clients they expect to locate there. In 1988 alone, the number of such plants grew by 45 percent, a record, and at this writing most observers expected that pace of expansion to continue.

Indeed, in mid 1989 the Mexican government further liberated its foreign investment laws to allow the development of even more *maquiladoras*, and executives of both the Touche Ross and Ernst & Young accounting firms publicly extolled the virtues of that decision.

At about the same time, Charlie Crowder, a New Mexico businessman, and the former mayor of the Mexican border city of Juarez were making plans to create a brand new border city of the future to be called "Santa Teresa." The new city would be the *maquiladora* capital of the world, located partially in the United States and partially in Mexico. Its economy would be based on the cheap Mexican labor trapped within its southern half, but Crowder envisioned making it more productive than other *maquiladora* developments by giving the workers a few more amenities. To assist him in his plans, Harvard University design classes drew up blueprints for Crowder's proposed new city.

"How can you be efficient," Crowder quipped to *Business Week*, "if you wake up with no plumbing, walk through a slum to work, and worry about your grandmother's safety?"

The enthusiasm of the business community for the *maquiladoras* is easy to understand. By setting up factories just a few yards outside America, manufacturers can conduct their financial and legal dealings within the relative political and legal stability of the United States, while cutting their labor costs to 20 percent or less of what they would have to pay Americans to do the same work.

The early *maquiladoras* were involved primarily in electronic parts assembly and textile production. But the twin-factory system has grown to include the assembly of such durables as kitchen appliances. And with thousands of acres of new *maquiladora* sites scheduled for development, it is logical to assume that an ever-widening array of products will be produced by the mills on the Mexican side as the 21st century debuts.

So the residents of Murua and similar border communities have an ever-growing supply of employment opportunities that promise to last a lifetime. What they lack, however, is the opportunity to earn substantial compensation for their labor—the kind of compensation that would allow them to escape their economic humiliation. To accomplish that, they would have to cross over to America and become citizens, or at least legal residents, and earn American-style wages. But, officially, America can't accept them.

Life Without Mexicans

It's not that America has nothing for the Mexicans to do within U.S. boundaries. Obviously, the American corporations that have invested in the *maquiladoras* have much work that needs to be done. And just a few miles north of the border the residents of Southern California's super-affluent beach towns can't figure out how to enjoy life *without* the labor of Mexicans.

For example, less than 24 hours before a trip to Murua in the summer of 1988, I heard numerous people at an elegant outdoor cocktail party in Laguna Beach bemoaning the fact that the U.S. government was cracking down harder than ever on their use of illegal Mexican immigrants as gardeners, domestic help and handymen.

For decades the system had worked like this: groups of Mexicans who had successfully circumvented the barriers America has established to keep them on their own side of the border would gather on street corners in Southern California in the morning. Californians with work to be done would drive up to one of those corners and select one or more Mexicans, offering them $4 or $5 an hour to trim their lawns and hedges, for example. At the end of the day the Mexicans would be paid and dropped off at their corner of origin.

For the Mexican workers the system was exploitive, but nonetheless resulted in a huge material improvement over the lifestyle of their native land, as well as an opportunity to work so long and hard that they would rise above the street-corner labor market. For Southern California's citizens, the system certainly beat doing the work oneself.

By mid 1988, however, the U.S. government had decided to crack down even harder on illegal immigration from Mexico. The warlike U.S. police activities designed to keep the Mexicans from coming over, under and through the fence that separates their country from the United States were no longer sufficient: The U.S. government began impounding the cars of Californians caught picking up "illegals" on street corners.

When such an impoundment occurred, it was heavily publicized so that it would serve as a deterrent to would-be employers of Mexicans who have entered America illegally. Apparently Washington knows that if there's anything that frightens a Southern Californian more than not being able to obtain cheap Mexican labor, it's losing his or her car.

The crackdown sent a shock through places such as Laguna Beach, and Californians began pondering how to live without Mexicans as servants. But some of California's more formally structured employers have suffered from this government-imposed shortage of Mexican workers as well. In some cases, the immigration restrictions have driven business organizations to economic absurdity.

For example, in 1988 Los Angeles apparel manufacturers petitioned the federal government for special permission to import 3,000 Filipino seamstresses to fill the void left by Mexican seamstresses scared away by increased immigration restriction enforcement. At the same time, California produce growers were considering the temporary importation of Chinese farm workers because they couldn't harvest their crops without all the Mexicans who used to find their way north to work on the farms.

Each year, the U.S. government spends millions more on keeping the Mexicans out. Each year businesses in the American West and Southwest spend many millions more—perhaps billions more—trying to replace the badly needed labor the Mexicans had provided. Each year an increasing number of American churches and human service organizations are finding themselves committing officially criminal acts because their consciences won't allow them to turn needy Mexicans away just because they lack the immigration credentials that would allow them to survive economically in America. And each year the residents of Laguna Beach become more perplexed over how to keep their gardens trimmed and their bathrooms clean.

Triangle of Confusion

Obviously a huge and increasingly expensive pool of confusion exists within the triangle formed by America's tradition of being a nation of immigrants, its contemporary policies and attitudes relating to immigration, and the needs of the U.S. workforce.

This high level of confusion was confirmed by a 1988 survey conducted in California by The Field Institute, a San Francisco-based, nonpartisan public policy research organization. California has usurped New York City's traditional position as America's principal port of entry for immigrants. Indeed, since California will eventually become the first state in the union in which white people of European descent are the minority, questions relating to the new arrivals are particularly important to California's governmental leaders. So the survey asked, in part, what effects California's citizens expect from the huge increases in the state's Hispanic and Asian populations that were developing in the '80s.

In regard to both Hispanics and Asians, the respondents overwhelmingly felt that the presence of the new immigrants would enhance the California workforce: 73 percent of the respondents said it was "very likely" that the growing Hispanic segment would provide "needed labor for new jobs," and 76 percent said the growing number of Asians in the population would have the same positive effect.

Yet, when the same respondents were asked what *negative* effects they expected from these same ethnic groups, a great conflict of opinion became evident: 77 percent felt that the Hispanics would cause an "increasing amount of unemployment in the state," and 60 percent predicted the same effect as a result of the growth of Asian population.

It is, of course, difficult to imagine how a person can represent a needed increase in the labor supply and a threat of increased unemployment at the same time. But the confusion doesn't end there.

At about the same time that The Field Institute was asking those questions about immigration, the City of Los Angeles was soliciting proposals for the design and creation of a world-class monument to rival the Statue of Liberty and celebrate Southern California's new status as the gateway to the Land of Immigrants. Meanwhile, in an area less than 150 miles south of Los Angeles, U.S. Border Patrol agents in cars, trucks and helicopters worked vigilantly to ensure that as few Mexicans and Central Americans as possible were making their way into America.

This confusion is also becoming increasingly apparent among America's most powerful news media. During one week in 1989, *U.S. News & World Report* published a three-page article that demonstrated in great detail why America needs *more* immigrants, while *Time* magazine's cover story had U.S. Secretary of State James Baker worrying about America being *plagued* with immigrants.

Baker—a multimillionaire lawyer whose favorite form of relaxation is using a shotgun to blast to death wild turkeys artificially lured into open areas by man-made feeding stations—took a *Time* reporter along on one of his frequent hunts, which he says provide him with a form of emotional therapy. Walking across a ranch in Texas, Baker found some emptied sardine cans.

"See those sardine cans?" Baker remarked. "The illegals have been by. They come through here and other spots on their way in. If we don't get a handle on Third World debt, we'll be overrun by Mexicans coming here to work. It's got to be one of our main priorities. . . ."

A few weeks later *The New York Times* celebrated St. Patrick's Day with a joyous editorial entitled "All Irish, All Immigrants." "One motto of today," it said in part, "is that on St. Patrick's Day, we're all Irish; another is that on St. Patrick's Day we're all immigrants. . . . Yes, they're celebrating a saint, but they're also celebrating a home. And the rest of us celebrate with them, honoring their home and ours. What a fortunate people we are, to be so rich in homes."

At the top of the front page of that day's editions of *The Times*, however, was a story about how the U.S. government had enlisted the help of the Mexican government in helping to keep Central Americans from entering America via the Mexican border. The editorial had not alluded to that situation, so it appears that on

St. Patrick's Day, everybody in America is Irish *except* immigrants from Central America. There is something about *their* home, apparently, that the Land of Immigrants does not wish to celebrate.

America's Sewer

There is, probably, no American who encounters the effects of America's confused attitudes and actions toward immigrants more often—or more personally—than the Rev. Joseph Langford, leader of a tiny band of young Roman Catholic priests headquartered in a small-but-growing mission in Murua.

Father Langford is head of the male members of Mother Teresa's Missionaries of Charity. When I met him in 1988 he was only 37, and his order was only five years old, but he had seen much of the worst that this world has to offer. Comprised of men from around the world who have been drawn to Mother Teresa's work, the order's charter is to work with the poorest of the earth's poor, and it's first formal mission was located in New York's infamous South Bronx.

By the summer of 1988, however, the order had moved its world headquarters to Tijuana's Murua, which some of the priests allude to as "Calcutta West" because of the wretchedness of the community's living conditions. Murua, they found, was in much greater need of charity than was the South Bronx.

Father Langford, a native of San Diego, left Southern California in 1969. He carried memories of Tijuana, the Mexican border city adjacent to his hometown, with him throughout his school years and his early years in the priesthood. In 1987, he recalls, he began to experience an inner drive to do something about the destitution of the laboring class of Tijuana. Those impoverished people had remained particularly vivid in his memories, and his memories were calling him back.

Shortly thereafter, Father Langford presented his feelings about Tijuana to Mother Teresa, and in May 1988 she and he toured the city for three days. After seeing the suffering of Murua, she agreed that the Missionaries of Charity should put their roots down there.

Despite his extensive experience with poverty, Father Langford still seemed awed one day in 1988 as he pointed from the mission yard to the hovels of Murua, to the people that he and fellow priests call "the neighbors."

"You can drive for 20 minutes and it just doesn't stop," he pointed out. "It's one thing to come down from an ivory tower, rub up against it for a while, and then go back and ponder what to do with these people. But you get such an incredibly deeper perspective when you walk through there. Babies are dying there because the water is so polluted—babies dying from amoebas in the water."

Older children and adults suffer in Murua, as well. Yet their resilience in the face of America's rejection is such that it surprises even the world-wise missionaries. For instance, one teenage daughter of a family that resides on the upper ridge of Murua contracted a waterborne disease that has left her with no control of her limbs. When the missionaries received two chickens as a gift, they decided to send one of their band up into the hills to give the chickens to that troubled family. The next day the crippled girl and her parents visited the mission to thank the priests.

"It must have taken her an hour to walk down from up there," Father Langford recalled with amazement. "And she did it on a set of crutches so beat up that you'd throw them away in the States."

The Missionaries of Charity work with the people of Murua and surrounding regions in an unstructured way. They wander among the homes listening to personal problems, trying to provide empathy and encouragement, and serving as ombudsmen in helping the families that inhabit the shacks to restructure their lives in whatever way they can. When the missionaries succeed in helping the families find work, it is often in the *maquiladoras*. The priests regard the *maquiladoras* as sweatshops and they make no attempt to hide their disdain for them. But they have pragmatically accepted the mills as the only available option.

In the process of helping the residents of Murua, the Missionaries of Charity have learned that their neighborhood's residents are virtually all economic refugees, people who left home destined for America. Unable to sustain themselves in their native communities, they set out for *El Norte* with hopes for a better life.

"These are people who tried to get across the border and didn't make it," said Father Langford. It hurts, he added, to see dozens of them line up along the drainage culvert near the border fence each evening to await nightfall and another opportunity to make a run for U.S. soil. "How many dreams are standing on the edge of that culvert?" he asked.

Most of the would-be Americans are from the central and southern regions of Mexico, but some have trudged all the way from Central America in the belief that they could enter the United States and find work. In many cases, they were misled by representatives of "coyotes," people who claim to sell safe passage into America.

"Maybe they saved up all their family's hard-earned money and took that precious treasure to pay the coyote and then got ripped off. Or maybe they got caught and dumped back over the border," Father Langford said.

"They've got no friends here, no work, no family—
nothing. They can't go back home because they have no
money to get back. If they move down into the city,
they're just going to get ripped off again—they're going
to have to get involved in prostitution or drugs or whatever."

The residents of Murua reside primarily in family
units. "All they have is a shack—you wouldn't put your
lawnmower in it back home—but for them it's a place to
live," Father Langford pointed out.

Most estimates in recent years place the number of
such refugees arriving at Tijuana's bus depot at a torren-
tial 2,000 per day, more than one-half million a year. By
the time they find their way to Father Langford's mission on the hill above the depot, most have been sub-
jected to an array of tricks, brutality and degradation.
They are easy prey for the street-wise criminals from
downtown Tijuana who use the bus station as their
base of operations. Often the patriarch of a family step-
ping off a bus is disabled by a punch or a blow from a
club, and the family's meager belongings are swiftly
stolen.

It is not unusual, the priests say, for a man to have
several ribs broken by muggers within minutes of his
family's arrival at Tijuana's bus station.

By the time the migrating families wander, defeated,
up into the adjacent hills of Murua, "they have deep
human and spiritual needs that they're not going to get
at a government feeding program—someone to sit
down and listen, someone to dry their tears, to talk
with them, pray with them, give them some sort of
hope in their life," said Father Langford. "Someone to
give them love and be witness in a world that has torn
them from family and everything they held dear. Someone to stand before them in the name of God's love."

About six months later, Jon and I returned to Murua to continue our research. This time, we were accompanied by Lourdes Regala, an actress and television documentary producer fluent in Spanish and exceptionally well prepared by her cultural background to win the confidence of Father Langford's neighbors. With her assistance, we were able to talk candidly at length with some of the people of Murua, and even to spend time in the simple homes they had constructed.

We were pleased to find that the Missionaries of Charity had already succeeded in expanding their mission to include a medical clinic and a pavillion-style church that filled beyond capacity on Sunday mornings with people who, despite the dust and mud, managed to dress up colorfully in their best go-to-church clothes. (The Murua mission chapel is, by the way, the only church I've ever visited that took no collection, nor had a receptacle into which one could drop money).

We were dismayed, however, to see that the size of the community had nearly doubled since our last visit—and, worse, that Mexican politicians had begun to exploit the situation.

The area on one side of the mission now had some water troughs and a few electrical service connections were being installed. But throughout that section the emblem of the ruling political party was now prominently displayed, making it quite clear to the residents that the politicians could, if they wanted to, alleviate some of the suffering.

On the other side of Murua there were no such improvements. The people there are, of course, members of the dissident party.

We also learned that some of the companies that own and run the *maquiladoras* had developed a way to hang a carrot on the end of a stick and dangle it before the people of Murua. Along one edge of the area covered by the hovels, the companies had constructed apartment complexes that resemble the low-income housing projects built by the federal government in the United States. Work three years in one *maquiladora* while living in a hovel—and have several children in the meantime—and you'll be granted the right to rent one of these company homes, the Muruans are told. Obviously, the owners of the *maquiladoras* have discovered the time-honored employment axiom that hungry babies will keep people tied down more securely than chains.

The only help that comes to the Muruans with no strings attached is that which comes from the missionaries and their supporters. For example, in the winter of 1989 Father Langford raised about $5,000 to purchase plastic tarpaulins which his team distributed, without political preference, to the people of Murua so that they could make the roofs of their hovels somewhat resistant to the winter rains.

Just before we arrived on our second visit, however, Father Langford's priests had encountered a particularly troubling problem with one of the new arrivals. A young woman had moved to Murua with no family to support her, little maternal experience and an infant so starved that when she laid the baby on the floor of her unfurnished shack, it ate dirt. The priests did what little they could, creating a hammock-like bed to keep the baby up off the ground and arranging for the woman to get some food from the supplies that they and the Missionaries of Charity regularly distribute to the families that need them most.

Like Mother Teresa, Father Langford works hard at being apolitical. That goal is not easy to attain, given his daily encounters. But his job, he explains, is to "convert hearts, not pass legislation." In his Sunday morning sermons, he repeatedly urges his parishioners not to become embittered or depressed, or to lose their faith in God or fellow human beings because of the oppression and exploitation they endure. He is unable, however, to hide his great displeasure with the resolve of his fellow Americans to maintain an artificial economic boundary between Mexico and America.

"We're responsible for creating this," he said to me one evening in the yard of the mission, gesturing toward the hovels of his neighbors. "We've been using them as our sewer for a long, long time. We're betraying who we are as immigrants, sons of immigrants and sons of sons of immigrants."

Looking out from the mission's yard, there is a temptation to romanticize Murua and the nearby border crossing at Otey Mesa as a potential modern-day version of New York's Ellis Island, the federal immigrant processing station through which millions of work-hungry European immigrants passed early in the 20th century to energize America's contemporary economy and create America's contemporary culture. But Father Langford quickly extinguishes that thought.

"Ellis Island was a place of hope. This is a place of despair," he said despondently. "We offer a little bit of hope in a sea of despair. Even in the barrios of Chicago, they're one hundred times better off.

"To turn this into a new Ellis Island would take the kind of policy that is written on the bottom of the Statue of Liberty. We should either cover that up, or do it.

"I'm sure that, if we have enough industry and genius to put people on the moon, we can find a way to put these people in some place like Wyoming," he said.

Places like Wyoming are not, however, a part of the

debate over America's immigration policies as the country prepares for the 21st century. Indeed, the debate has virtually ignored such issues as geographic distribution and overall labor market needs.

The enormity and complexity of the issue of American attitudes toward immigrants has not diminished, however. In the mid 1980s the number of people wishing to immigrate to America began to approach that of the 1920s, when millions of impoverished people flooded to America's eastern shores from Europe. By 1989 at least 700,000 immigrants per year were entering America, legally and illegally.

What's more, the atrocities that frequently befall those desperate people who attempt to enter America illegally were beginning to make news in parts of the country far removed from the Mexican border—where such events have become, tragically, routine.

For example, in early 1989 four Asians, including a seven-year-old child, drowned in the Niagara River while apparently being smuggled from Ontario, Canada, into New York State aboard a flimsy raft. Benedict J. Ferro, district director of the U.S. Immigration and Naturalization Service for that region, told The New York Times that such smugglings were new to his jurisdiction, but that his staff had begun investigating small-boat crossings several months before and had apprehended eleven Chinese who had succeeded in making their way from Canada to the U.S. by boat.

A few weeks later, six Salvadorans were discovered in a railroad boxcar in Kansas City, Missouri. They had been attempting to reach Washington, D.C., where a relative had promised they could find work and a place to reside. They had been living in below-freezing temperatures for several days on a gallon of milk. By the time police found them, two of the Salvadorans had to be hospitalized for frostbite on their feet and legs.

Despite the horrors endured by many would-be immigrants, resistance to immigrants was beginning to grow more ugly. For example, in February 1989 the Southern Poverty Law Center, an organization focusing on civil rights legislation based in Montgomery, Alabama, warned that white-supremacist organizations were being rejuvenated in America by the emergence of gangs of neo-Nazi American youths.

The members of the gangs are known as "skinheads" because of their short-cropped hair. In 1988, the report said, skinheads had been connected with killings in Portland, Oregon; San Jose, California; Reno and Las Vegas, Nevada. Most of the incidents had been random attacks on blacks, Hispanics, Asians or homosexuals.

Also in early 1989 the U.S. Immigration and Naturalization Service (INS) began digging a trench four miles long, fourteen feet wide and five feet deep across the flatlands of Otey Mesa to further ensure the inability of the people of Murua to escape to the side of the border where their employers reside.

And at the same time America's resolve to deport Nicaraguans, Salvadorans and other Central Americans trying to enter America through Texas grew to the point where Mexican officials complained that they were apprehending people trying to swim across the Rio Grande in attempts to escape from America to Mexico.

And, perhaps most ironically, the INS decided in 1989 to build a prison to hold undocumented aliens on a reservation in San Diego, California, that had been set aside for the Viehas band of Mission Indians. Now America's newest residents are being imprisoned on the land of those who have been in America the longest.

Only the Best and Brightest

In response to the growing pressure at America's gate and the growing fears and resentments surrounding immigrants, U.S. political leaders have conducted lengthy discussions of legislation that would significantly alter the prevailing post-World War II policy of allowing people to enter legally primarily on the basis of family ties to existing American citizens.

However, the most-discussed alternative has been that of accepting only the most highly educated and skilled immigrants, the cream of the world's workforce, and people who have money to invest in American businesses—those people who, in a global context, are least in need of a chance to move up economically. Consequently, neither the people of Murua nor their opportunity-seeking brethren from other parts of the Third World—today's equivalents of the economic adventurers from Europe who surged through Ellis Island—are being actively considered for admission.

Certainly immigration has been a controversial matter in America for centuries. But why is it that America is no longer a place that asks the world to send "your tired, your poor, your huddled masses yearning to breathe free," the "wretched refuse of your teeming shores"? Why does it cherish its image as a nation of up-from-the-mud immigrants, and yet fear the arrival of new waves of impoverished peoples?

Why has America developed into a society that is willing to see hordes of people suffer in the shadow of its affluence because of its immigration restrictions? Why is it unwilling to allow entry to those who would gladly do the jobs that Americans reject as too menial and poorly compensated, yet is prepared to welcome those people who are equipped to move almost immediately to the top of the American economic scale—further crowding the career ladders that native Americans and their children wish to climb and further exacerbating resentment of ambitious immigrants?

Most research on immigration attitudes shows, ironically, that fear of Americans losing their employment opportunities to newcomers is the simple-yet-prevalent motivation for contemporary government restrictions on immigration. If America were to open its shores to all who would come, Americans have come to believe, their jobs would be endangered.

But would that really be the case? Do fears of mass immigration have a basis in fact? Is it somehow better to receive extensively educated people with high career aspirations than those whose lack of education and economic underpinnings make them eager to do whatever work needs to be done? Does the Statue of Liberty, by lifting its lamp "beside the golden door," invite economic hardship for existing Americans?

The Allure of "Jobilism"

Like many economists, Richard B. McKenzie, a professor at Clemson University and author of *The American Job Machine* (Universe Books, 1988), contends that fears of mass immigration are largely unfounded. He takes the point a step farther, however, by showing that fears of immigrants are part of a very serious and much larger contemporary problem in America that he calls "jobilism."

"Jobilism is a dogmatic protection of jobs for the sake of the protection of jobs," McKenzie explains. "It's a philosophical bent that believes that jobs, in and of themselves, are terribly important.

"The jobilists believe that the purpose of an economy

is to create jobs. In fact, that's the easiest task an economy has. All you need to do, for example, to create 60 million jobs is to abolish farm machinery."

Nurtured by the economic tumult of America's transition from the Industrial Era to the Information Age, jobilism became the most influential dogma of American public policy in the 1980s. The build-up of labor in Murua is but one symbol of jobilism's pervasive influence.

Waving the same banner of jobilism, for example, huge and very profitable corporations have won immense tax abatements from cities that are barely able to meet their police and firefighter payrolls. In the name of jobilism, various levels of federal and state governments have paid tens of millions of dollars to foreign companies to train Americans to perform manufacturing jobs in their U.S. factories. Indeed, even huge auto factories have been built at government expense because, the companies that utilize the factories have successfully argued, such commercial diversions of public money save America's most valued resource, jobs.

The degree to which America has adopted jobilism as its contemporary economic creed was emphasized, unintentionally, by President George Bush when, in accepting the Republican presidential nomination in the summer of 1988, he promised to create 30 million new jobs in four years—even though his own economists agreed that the United States could, at best, only provide about half that many workers from within its borders. The rest of the world laughed, but in America the jobilism faith was undamaged and Bush was elected.

While America pursues jobilism with fervor, Professor McKenzie points out, global trends are quickly making its jobilism-inspired immigration restrictions obsolete—and the suffering of such places as Murua unnecessary.

"New technologies are making these immigration laws irrelevant," he says. "To the extent that there is any usefulness in immigration restrictions, technology is obliterating that usefulness.

"Technology is going to break down the immigration barriers. If you try to keep people out, then you'll just have capital going to the labor. If you don't let people in to produce goods at low wages, then the work can go to them.

"It used to be that the mobility of capital was restricted by the cost of transportation and communication. But I can now send production orders from the computer in the office in my home in the Carolinas. If people want to restrict Mexicans from coming in, I can just as easily send production orders to Cancun as I can to a plant six miles from here," he says.

"We want to bar immigration by not allowing the person to come in. But when you can communicate with a worker in Cancun as well as you can one in North Carolina, they are effectively in the country anyway. Telecommunication has, in effect, allowed a lot of people in without them actually coming here. People don't have to come here anymore to get work. You can ship it to them at the speed of light, and at the cost of light."

As an example, Professor McKenzie cites the fact that a number of American banks employ check-processing facilities in the Caribbean. The checking account data is entered by low-cost Caribbean keyboard operators, and the information is then transmitted back to the United States via advanced telecommunications technologies, such as optical fibers and satellite transmissions. The keyboard operators haven't entered America, but their labor has.

Perhaps more important, he points out, is the fact that there is little logic—and a great deal of international embarrassment—in Americans coveting the low-skill jobs that many impoverished immigrants would fill. "If Americans have to fend off through immigration restrictions people from the Third World who have extraordinarily limited educations, Americans are not going to have very high incomes anyway," he says.

Honoring "Ethnic Pop"

There is, however, one huge difference between tele-communicating work to impoverished countries and allowing the people of those countries to immigrate legally to America. Allowed to enter and pursue citizenship, if they wish, such immigrants would no longer be imprisoned for life by the economic short-comings of their native lands. Like millions before them they would have the freedom to work hard, move up and pursue what Americans proudly call the "American Dream"—a concept that is as essential to the country's self-image as the Stars and Stripes.

The immigrants would also have the opportunity, as did the Irish who first settled in New England, to over-come—at least to a tolerable extent—exploitation by corrupt and entrenched politicians through the democratic process, eventually taking control of their own political destiny. What's more, they would have the opportunity to reprove one of the least-known economic axioms: that prosperity follows where immigrants go.

Such was the case in the early part of the 20th century. America held open its golden door, millions of economic refugees flooded in past the Statue of Liberty, and the most powerful economy on earth was born.

Economic historians point out that had that huge immigration not occurred, America probably would not have become the industrial leader of the world—nor would it have had the industrial strength that supported its victories in World War II and kept the war away from its shores. Indeed, about half of the people who make up America's workforce today, myself included, wouldn't be here if it hadn't been for that huge mass immigration that brought their parents, grandparents and great-grandparents to America.

Ben Wattenberg of The American Enterprise Institute makes a very succinct argument that reinforces this point: If the huge immigration to America that took place just before and after the start of the 20th century had been restricted in the way that many Americans desire today, America's contemporary global economic influence would be about equal to that of Australia.

That very strong connection between the availability of inexpensive immigrant labor and the 20th century prosperity of America's manufacturers is rarely discussed outside academic circles. Indeed, I find that even some of the most highly educated Americans I talk with in the course of my writing have never read or heard of that connection.

Nevertheless, the contribution of the early-20th century immigrants to the cultural abundance of contemporary American life has become such an essential component of the fabric of America that novelist Philip Roth, best known for *Portnoy's Complaint*, has given a name to the school of U.S. politics that exploits the American affection for immigrant imagery. He calls it "Ethnic Pop." Roth points out politicians such as New York Governor Mario Cuomo and Massachusetts Gover-

nor Michael Dukakis have won elections because they
have become masters of Ethnic Pop.

"There is no indignation in Ethnic Pop," Roth wrote
in an essay for *The New York Times,* "no shame, no
self-hatred, no loathing—there is only pride and gratitude. The harsher the conditions under which the father suffered in the new country, the more love there is
for both father and country. And there is no failure that
is tragic or ruinous: For every father who may have been
martyred, mangled or crushed, there is, to redeem him,
an estimable success of a son."

This image of the humble-but-hard-working immigrant who finds success in America is a keystone of the
manner in which most Americans view themselves,
and understandably so. There are millions of Americans living today who have experienced exactly that
type of economic transition. Yet this is an image that
obviously collides with contemporary socioeconomic
values and beliefs. Through a series of sad circumstances, Americans have learned to see hungry-to-work
immigrants more as a newly arrived problem than as a
newly gained asset.

At the beginning of the 20th century, America's economy welcomed impoverished immigrants as a fresh
crew of badly needed helpers. Less than 100 years later,
however, it feels a need to defend against the immigrants as though they are soldiers of the enemy.

New Face in the Mirror

The people who populate such places as Murua are,
therefore, but one facet of a much larger story, and the
conflicts over immigration that are being played out in
immigration-conscious places such as California,
Miami and South Texas are merely part of a sweeping

international drama that is touching—or will soon touch—every citizen and community in America and many outside of it. It is a drama that is in no way limited to Mexicans, Central Americans, Asians, or any other ethnic group. As technology makes the world smaller and smaller, this drama will be played out on a huge, global stage.

Its resolve to keep many newcomers out notwithstanding, America is rapidly approaching the time when its citizens will no longer be able to recognize only those persons whose physical appearance derives from European genes as real Americans, as has been the case through most the past three centuries.

Since most modern-day immigrants are coming from Hispanic and Asian countries, Americans' physical perception of themselves is being challenged. More than ever, America is becoming an ethnic and racial rainbow, and the populace is quickly losing its ability to divide itself neatly into the Industrial Era categories of white and black. More than ever before, America is becoming a country that has no indigenous genetic identity.

The *Los Angeles Times* emphasized this fact in a very entertaining way on Feb. 14, 1989. Nearly all American newspapers have made a tradition of publishing some type of romance-related story on page one to observe Valentine's Day, and the *Los Angeles Times* is no exception. But its love story for 1989 was one that certainly would have shocked all of America two decades ago, and would probably still horrify many people in less liberal areas of America.

"Mixed Marriages Keep Pace with L.A. Diversity," said the headline. The story cited numerous sources of statistics to demonstrate that people in Los Angeles were marrying across racial, ethnic and religious lines in dramatically increasing numbers. For example, UCLA sociologist Harry H. L. Kitano had studied the last names and birthplaces on marriage certificates to ascertain that in 1984 more than half of all Japanese marrying in Los Angeles had married someone who had a background other than Japanese. Other researchers had discovered such trends as Mexican women marrying men of other backgrounds to escape the rigid Mexican traditions that tend to keep wives on a plane lower than their husbands.

That Valentine's Day story reminded me of an incident I had experienced that demonstrates, by contrast, how rapidly America's attitudes toward such mixing are changing. Only about five years earlier, I had come to know an Asian-born woman in Cleveland who had been prevented by racial prejudice from becoming part of mainstream America. She was a very energetic and highly skilled worker, but racial barriers had prevented her from earning enough money to support herself.

Cleveland has long been one of the most racist cities in America, a place where, in her youth, this Asian-American woman was not allowed to socialize in prosperous circles. So, out of desperation, she married an uneducated, unskilled, ghetto-dwelling, alcoholic black man—a victim of similar racist standards—who had found his economic resting place on the payroll of the U.S. Postal Service. He wasn't much, but he paid the rent.

Because of their clashing values, their life together was one of stress and violence. People who saw her arriving punctually for work each day downtown, beautifully dressed and impeccably groomed, couldn't believe the truth about her existence: That she went home each night to a neighborhood where an unshattered window was rare—and to a man who spent his days watching pornographic videotapes in a drunken stupor, and then imagining that his wife was enjoying similar sexual adventures with other men.

She tried a few times to escape that marriage of necessity. But in places such as Cleveland, a sophisticated Asian woman still is often regarded as an oddity roughly equal to a talking dog, so she had no avenue of escape. One day she didn't report to work at the designated time, and her supervisor received a call from the police shortly thereafter. The night before, the police said, her jealousy-wracked husband had ordered her into their bedroom and, after ordering their son to watch, used a pistol to blow her brains out.

Although the demise of the racial standards that forbade "mixed" marriages with members of the more affluent racial and ethnic groups—and sentenced that innocent lady to a bullet in the head—may be occurring most dramatically and documented most assiduously in Southern California, the demise is by no means limited to that region. Consequently, opinions on who should and should not be allowed to enter the United States and pursue the American Dream soon will be going through great waves of revision, and it is logical to expect a great clashing of interests and emotions as those waves pass.

There will be a new face in America's mirror, and its collective perspective will be altered: The plight of those Mexicans standing on the edge of Tijuana's drainage culvert can seem much more outrageous when their faces resemble those of your spouse's brothers and sisters. The practice of exploiting Asian sweat labor in Taiwan to assemble televisions cheaply for the American marketplace is much less acceptable when your husband or wife—and consequently, your son or daughter—has jet-black hair and eyes that are, by European standards, slanted.

About nine million immigrants, double the number that entered the United States in the 1970s and most much different in physical appearance than those who arrived in the earlier parts of the 20th century, moved to American during the 1980s. And although that rate was much less, as a percentage of the U.S. population, than during the peak years of immigration in the period 1900 to 1930, the '80s saw more immigration to America than any other decade since World War I.

What's more, the pressure to find a better place to live was increasing in other parts of the world. A 1988 report by the Council of Europe estimated the working-age population of the world's poorest and most troubled countries was increasing by 60 million people annually. A large percentage of those people want to move, and are likely to attempt to move, to more prosperous countries in the 1990s and in the early decades of the 21st century. The study also projected that their need to become newcomers to foreign lands would be made more urgent by "human rights violations in 130 of the world's 170 nations, and 40 armed conflicts around the globe."

Nevertheless, in the absence of the huge percentages of young immigrant labor that energized it during the Industrial Era, America's population is aging, raising the frightening possibility of the creation of a society unable to support itself economically or even militarily. "I think we're going to face serious economic trouble in our desperate attempts to sustain a welfare state," Rockford Institute president Alan C. Carlson told *The New York Times* in 1989. "It will be difficult to defend our immediate security needs as a larger and larger portion of the country's gross national product is consumed by the cost of healthcare for an aging population."

It would be difficult—indeed, depressing—to believe that in the face of such long-term, heartfelt conflicts and influences, simplistic rules allowing only the world's most highly educated and well-financed people to enter America will be accepted as the best and final solution—that the Land of Immigrants will be forever willing to abide Longfellow's 19th century observation that "One half the world must sweat and groan, that the other half may dream."

So whether your viewpoint is one born of humanism, economic self-interest, politics, romantic experiences, military security concerns or simply sentimentality, America's contemporary attitudes and policies regarding immigrants beg for reexamination and contemplation. What has worked in the past certainly won't work in the future. America's attitudes toward immigrants have long been confused, continue to be confused, and are becoming even more so.

Despite its immigrant roots and the profound economic effect that earlier waves of immigration had, America has never enacted an immigration policy based on economic information and logic; at best, its immigration laws have been amalgamations of petty special interests and politically expedient compromises. At worst, they are codifications of fear, prejudice and hatred.

So let's look in the chapters that follow at how the people of the United States arrived at the assumption that immigration to America should be limited and controlled; who benefitted and who didn't from immigration restrictions; how jobilism and other factors have colored attitudes toward those who would become Americans, and at the motivations and positions of interests that already are fighting to change contemporary immigration restrictions.

Let's also consider what the prospects are for America's door to swing wide once again, and how a return to America's earlier, more open immigrant traditions would affect Americans personally, nationally and as a part of the increasingly open world economy.

CHAPTER 2

A Brief History of American Immigrant Rivalries

S ITTING ACROSS THE DESK from me was a very beau-
tiful young woman who spoke English with a very
slight foreign accent that was not easy to classify. Her
long, jet-black hair and honey-colored skin indicated
she might be from Mexico or South America. But we
were in Los Angeles, America's preeminent ethnic and
racial melting pot of the late 20th century. It was De-
cember and we were talking about what all our business associates would be doing during the Christmas
holiday season, and especially about which of them
would be going back to their hometowns for the holi-
days.

Rather than make an assumption that had a high risk
of being incorrect, I asked where "home" was for her.
She had been born in Burma, she explained. But Los

Angeles had become home to her because virtually all of her immediate family had moved to America.

Why had they decided to move to America? I asked.

Pushing herself back away from her desk and deeper into her chair, she looked askance at me as if I had just spoken in a language she didn't understand. She hesitated a few moments, then leaned forward and looked at me sternly.

"Just take a look around the world," she said with a sweeping hand motion and some condescension in her voice. "It's easy to see that this is the best place."

For her and her family it had been that simple. They had been business owners in their native land and had amassed enough money to buy the legal advice, political influence and air fares necessary to move easily to America. Like many other affluent people of the late 20th century from around the world, they saw no sense in moving to anywhere in America except California, where the weather is utopian and there are plenty of nice places and activities on which to spend your money year 'round.

However, the Garden-of-Eden syndrome of which they are a part represents only a minuscule segment of American immigration, past and present. Throughout the country's history, the great majority of decisions to move to America—the mass migrations that have had profound effects on the American economy and culture—have been part of an effort to escape economic hardship, not to find a culture that could accommodate and further enhance material wealth.

Even today, hundreds of thousands of people, who have never had the opportunity to travel around the world and decide which venue is best move to America each year simply because they have heard through the village grapevine that their chances of living a reasonably comfortable, satisfying and long life would be dramatically better in the Land of Immigrants.

For the most part, those who have moved to America have been economic scrappers. In most instances they were allowed into America simply because their labor was needed as a catalyst that would allow America's abundant stocks of natural resources, capital and technology to be synthesized into things that people needed or wanted. But despite the fact that they represented a most valuable economic resource, most immigrants have received—enroute to America and after arrival—treatment that has more often than not been cruel.

Consequently, the history of the relationships of America's immigrant groups with one another is riddled with rivalries. The wounds of cruelty heal slowly, if ever. So despite the nearly forty years of material affluence in America that followed World War II, many of those rivalries remain unresolved. The story of immigration to America and the rivalries that evolved from it is not a pretty one. Romanticism aside, it is a story that illustrates dramatically the brutality that can, and still does, arise from economic ignorance.

To a great extent the history of America's immigrant rivalries can be summed up with the chorus of an old British pub song:

It's the same, the whole world over,
It's the poor what gets the blame,
It's the rich gets all the pleasure,
Ain't it all a bloomin' shame.

What differentiates the United States from the socio-economically stratified birthplace of that song, however, is the fact that in America the poor often work their way up to being rich. These newly rich then utilize their new status to blame all sorts of problems on the people who took their place at the bottom of the heap.

The Conquering Immigrants

Whether or not the arrival of the people whom most Americans today know as "American Indians" (and to whom many people now refer as "Native Americans," even though that creates still further confusion over what to call people of other genetic backgrounds who also were born in America) should be included in a recounting of American immigrant waves is a question best left to anthropologists.

However, the subjugation of the Indians in contemporary America is, without question, due to the fact that their ancestors were grossly outnumbered by, and culturally and technologically unequipped to compete with, the sophisticated empire-builders who sailed from Europe to dominate the New World, and the small bands of early immigrants that followed them.

Tragic though the fate of American Indians has been, their experiences have little similarity to the other immigrant rivalries of the past two centuries. The world in which the Indians and the newcomers clashed was one of primarily nomadic and agrarian lifestyles, one that preceded the centralization and mechanization of work that provided much of the motivation for mass immigrations to America. And in direct contrast to the later waves of immigrants attracted by the Industrial Revolution and its aftermath, the newcomers from Europe who invaded the lands of the American Indian quickly became the group in control of the country and its economic resources.

So the early European settlers of America were not immigrants in the contemporary sense of the term. They were emissaries of foreign royalty, religious iconoclasts, entrepreneurs, adventurers, intellectuals, military leaders. They supplied the sophistication that created the concept of America. They were the keystones of the political and economic powers that formed what we know as the United States of America, and they stood high above subsequent arrivals who represented little more than quantities of the one commodity essential to industrialization that was not available locally, the commodity of human sweat.

The first mass immigration of mere human laborers to America was, ironically, the one that today still generates the greatest of rivalries among American ethnic groups. It took the form of blacks, most of them captured in Africa and brought to America against their will.

Often they were brought to America by sea captains who, regarding blacks as something less than humans, callously utilized the Africans merely as ballast for their ships. After delivering cargoes of raw materials such as lumber from America to the newly industrializing cities of Europe, the captains needed some other commodity to weigh down and stabilize the hulls of their sail-driven ships on the return trip to America to pick up more goods. A mariner could use rocks or some other such commodity as ballast, but the black-skinned humans captured in Africa were the only form of ballast that could be forced to carry itself on board, and that would eagerly move itself back out of the ship upon arrival at the next port.

The brutality of this system was such that one weathered British slave-ship captain became suddenly sickened by it while enroute from Africa, turned his ship around, let his human cargo run back onto their native soil, returned to England and retired from the sea. Shortly thereafter, to record his profound personal experience, he sat down and penned the timeless lyrics to "Amazing Grace."

The first blacks arrived in America in 1619 and became not unpaid slaves but indentured servants who could earn their way out of bondage, and that was the standard for several decades afterward. Eventually, those first black laborers became free people, and some of them ended up owning farms or businesses—and even unpaid black slaves.

As the 18th century approached, however, the demand for large quantities of inexpensive, easily controlled human labor began to grow, particularly among the owners of America's burgeoning plantations of the South. Just as they were considered to be a near-perfect form of ship ballast, blacks were considered perfect for the role of lifetime unpaid slave: They were easily identified by skin color among the European expatriates who controlled America, and they usually arrived on American soil without the English language skills or other personal attributes that would have allowed them to overcome their well-armed and entrenched captors. What's more, there was no powerful African government ready to protest such treatment of its subjects, as would have been the case if British subjects had been treated similarly.

During the 18th century, 200,000 blacks were imported to the American colonies and were put to work primarily as unpaid slaves on plantations in the South. Tragically, that region became an economic prison for most of them and their descendants for about two centuries.

However, in 1808 the importation of slaves to America was outlawed, primarily because of moral objections from Americans in the North, and that created a major problem for the new country under development.

Irish Replace the Africans

The many ships carrying raw materials from America to Europe's factories still needed ballast to remain upright in the winds on the trip back to the New World. But they could no longer take care of that problem by filling their holds with black Africans. At the same time, America, like Europe, was beginning to industrialize. It was building an infrastructure of canals, roads, bridges and aquaducts that would eventually nurture and support the factories, mills and mines of the Industrial Revolution, and it needed more and more human labor to accomplish those tasks. Horses and mules could pull the carts and plows, but it took the dexterity of a human to hit a spike with a mallet or run a log through a sawmill.

Also at the same time, an American tradition was taking shape: with the exception of the unpaid slaves, people who had been in the country for some time began moving up the economic ladder and began eschewing simple manual labor.

"Manpower had been scarce in America since the founding of Jamestown (in 1607), but it was becoming nonexistent as native men sought property of their own in the newly opened Western territories," notes Barbara Kaye Greenleaf in *America Fever: The Story of American Immigration* (Four Winds Press, 1970). "In any case, American men simply would not do pick-and-shovel work, which they felt was beneath them. Faced with the problem of large projects and few workers, construction companies followed the example of colonial employers: they turned to Europe."

Specifically, the companies and the ship captains turned to Ireland, which in the early 1800s was in the midst of a population explosion that threatened the existence of many of its inhabitants. Hungry, desperate Irish Africans were soon substituted for Africans as ballast in the holds of the ships returning to America. The ships were once again able to remain stiff in the wind, the Irish were equally good at unloading themselves, so the New World's first mass importation of Caucasian labor was born.

These workers from Ireland couldn't be choosey about their work as were the indigenous white residents of America. The Irish weren't as suitable for unpaid slavery, but dropped ashore, they needed a way—any way—to earn a living. Consequently, they were highly motivated and performed exceedingly well as laborers in the American economy for about three decades. In the process, they paved the way for millions who would follow them. Then, in 1845, the infamous potato famine struck Ireland, forcing many more people to begin fleeing to the States. By 1864, two and a half million Irish had moved to America and were hard at work doing America's hand labor.

The developed land and industries of early America were owned primarily by the British families and companies that had first settled the colonies, so the Irish, like the Mexicans today in Tijuana's Murua, gathered into hovel communities. Indeed, the similarity of the living conditions of nineteenth-century Irish-Americans to those of contemporary Mexican-U.S. border towns is startling. Despite the passage of more than a century and a half, the fate of the person willing to do America's hand labor has changed little.

The Irish "threw together shantytowns of discarded boxes and timbers on vacant lots near factories or on the outskirts of towns . . . ," notes Greenleaf. "These tenements were the breeding grounds for all kinds of diseases, and an observer noted that in the worst neighborhoods no one lived to have gray hairs."

Yet, despite their humbled status, the Irish began to be resented by those who had arrived before them. In Boston newspapers, employment ads began to carry an ending notation "NINA," meaning "no Irish need apply." In nearby Cambridge, two parallel horsecar lines were built: one for proper people to ride, and the other to carry the Irish to and from work.

At approximately the same time that the Irish began their mass move to America, Germany—which had already been industrialized to a great extent—was undergoing the effects of a severe economic depression and consequently political upheaval. By 1853, about one million economically displaced German immigrants had entered America, and in the decade that followed, the Germans and Irish arrived in nearly equal numbers. Together the two groups represented more than two-thirds of all legal immigration to the United States during the mid-1800s.

French Canadians were also immigrating to America then, drawn primarily by the availability of work in New England's textile mills, but their numbers never approached those of the Irish and Germans. Nevertheless, the three immigrant groups soon began to share the resentment and hatred of those who had arrived before them.

"With them the Irish, Germans and French Canadians brought their customs, language and religion (primarily Catholicism)," observed Vernon M. Briggs, Jr., a labor economist with Cornell University, in his superbly researched book *Immigration Policy and the American Labor Force* (Johns Hopkins University Press, 1984). "Among the numerically dominant Anglo-Saxon and strongly Protestant citizens of the urban Northeast, a nativist reaction set in. It took the form of verbal assaults on Catholicism and political radicalism in general, and on the personal characteristics of the new immigrants in particular. . . . Fierce debates were conducted in various state legislatures and in Congress over the desirability of unrestricted immigration and the unregulated naturalization of such ethnic groups."

Protestant clergymen and journalists in America fed the anti-Catholic sentiment, and a secret society known as the Order of the Star-Spangled Banner was formed with the goal of restricting immigration from non-Anglo-Saxon countries. Members were told to answer questions about the society with the words "I know nothing about it," so it eventually became known as the "Know Nothing Movement."

"The movement struck a responsive cord among workingmen who felt threatened with economic competition from the new immigrants," Briggs notes. "Other persons felt that Catholicism represented a genuine threat to American institutions. These feelings became the springboard for opportunistic politicians who were searching for a cause that would get them elected."

At about the same time, similar resentments were building on America's West Coast. During the 1850s more than 40,000 Asian immigrants moved into California, primarily to work on the construction of railroads. Although their absolute numbers were not large in comparison to the mass immigrations coming in via the East Coast, the Asians were quite noticeable by skin color and bodily configuration in the then-sparsely populated State of California. Consequently a number of anti-Asian state tax laws, such as a head tax on Chinese immigrants, were passed during that period.

The Civil War in the 1860s tended to distract people from their pursuit of immigrant rivalries, and in 1864 the Congress—by then controlled by Northern industrialists in need of human labor to fuel their new factories—even passed a law that allowed companies to recruit foreign workers and pay their transportation to America while encumbering the workers' wages for a year or more after their arrival to assure repayment of the fare.

From the end of the civil war until the mid 1880s the second great immigration of human labor to America occurred, most coming to the East Coast again from Germany, Ireland and England. Chinese were still coming to the West Coast, however, and now the railroads the Chinese had helped to build were bringing European immigrants from the port cities of the East to California. Almost immediately, a new type of immigrant rivalry erupted: the immigrants from Europe began to blame the Chinese for wage scales that the Europeans considered too low.

From that clash of immigrant interests came two mainstays of the organized labor movement that are still very much alive in America today: the "union label" and campaigns to induce Americans to buy only those goods that carry such a label. The first "union label" appeared on cigars made in San Francisco in 1872 and was white—its color symbolizing to concerned purchasers that the cigars had been made by Caucasian workers, not the allegedly wage-busting Asians.

Today, more than a century later, "union label" campaigns are conducted via prime-time television advertising in America and, although they would never admit it, the sponsors are in essence promulgating the same subtle racist message. For example, when the unions went on strike against Miami-based Eastern Airlines in 1989, asking the American public to boycott the airline in support of their fight in the spirit of organized labor, the faces of the headquarters picketers were predominantly white. Yet Miami is a city where white people—"Anglos" in the vernacular of Miami—are a minority.

Self-Perpetuating Poverty

It is also important to note that a syndrome of self-perpetuating poverty engulfed and tormented the America's industrial-era immigrants, much as it has the people of Murua.

America in the latter half of the 19th century was not a good place in which to be a wage worker. The factories and the concept of centralized work that the factories represented were in their infancy, and were not well managed. Yet they were sucking in America's economic resources at an unprecedented rate. Unlike contemporary Americans, people went to work in the factories not because they wanted to, but because they were left no alternative; the mechanization and centralization of work and the resultant productivity-increasing effects were making independent craftsmanship and small-scale agricultural pursuits obsolete.

No one had long-term experience managing a factory, however, so wage schedules were a matter of experimentation that was usually conducted with the immigrant laborer as the guinea pig. More often than not, the goal of the pay scale experiments was to see how low a wage one could pay and still get the goods out.

Under such conditions, the waves of immigrants usually found themselves sentenced to a life of squalor and insecurity. They kept their sanity by maintaining Old World cultural traditions in the company of fellow immigrants, by focusing on the goal of a better life for their children and, in many cases, regularly consuming large amounts of anesthetizing alcohol.

Then, as now, the indigenous population of America reversed the true cause-and-effect relationship, blaming the typical lifestyle of an immigrant on the genetic nature of the immigrant. Because they were perceived as troubled and unsophisticated people, immigrant laborers were excluded from most economic opportunities that the American culture reserved for untroubled people, and the immigrants' poverty became self-perpetuating.

"The spectacle of a class of men and women set apart by their social and economic disarray presented frightening problems . . . ," observed Syracuse University historian David H. Bennett in his book on the American nativist movement entitled The Party of Fear (University of North Carolina Press, 1988).

The nativists depicted the immigrants of the mid-19th century as a threat to the American way of life, he points out. "Who would want to live among the dangerous and diseased, the slothful and violent masses creating blight wherever they settled? Dealing in themes that would endure beyond the mid-nineteenth century, [the nativists] tried to elevate their movement beyond simple bigotry or economic self-interest. They fused the enduring image of a promised land to the fearful image of destructive intruders and fashioned for themselves a role as protectors of the American dream."

In the 1870s and 1880s, the American economy suffered two prolonged recessions that further aggravated the discontent of native Americans with the existing economic order. What's more, most of the jobs being created by America's fledgling manufacturing industries required primarily sweat labor and few skills, so a newly arrived immigrant could perform them nearly as well as one who had been in America for a while.

Consequently, by 1885 anti-immigrant sentiment had grown so strong that the federal government adopted a law that prohibited any person or business from assisting financially, or encouraging in any other way, the immigration of foreign workers under contract arrangements. Several states also began attempting to restrict immigration. America's highly structured employment market had begun to shape itself through the erection of economic barriers, and the barrier to immigration was one of the first to go up.

Perhaps the most poignant moment in all of America's history of immigrant rivalries occurred the following year when a 152-foot-high copper statue of a robed female holding a torch aloft was dedicated to commemorate the 100th anniversary of the Declaration of Independence. Erected on a small island in New York Harbor, it was a gift from the government of France and subsequently became known, of course, as the "Statue of Liberty."

On its base was inscribed an emotion-filled poem that Emma Lazarus, a Jewish-American immigrant from Russia, had written as part of the fund-raising efforts for erection of the statue:

> Give me your tired, your poor,
> Your huddled masses yearning to breathe free,
> The wretched refuse of your teeming shore,

Send these, the homeless, tempest-tossed to me:
I lift my lamp beside the golden door!

Contemporary America has romanticized that event to the point that it is remembered as one of national celebration. Indeed, the gala U.S. Bicentennial observance in 1976 was focused on the symbolism of the Statue of Liberty. And in 1989 the American news media enthusiastically reported the fact that democracy proponents in several Asian countries had erected replicas of the statue as part of their protests against existing governments. But, in truth, the statue was erected at a time when resentment and fear of immigrants were reaching historic highs in the United States.

"The dedication ceremonies for the Statue of Liberty in October 1886 took place, ironically enough, at precisely the time that Americans were beginning seriously to doubt the wisdom of unrestricted immigration," wrote Maldwyn Allen Jones, a professor of history at several leading universities, in his book *American Immigration* (University of Chicago Press, 1960). "In the prevailing atmosphere, Emma Lazarus's poetic welcome to the Old World's 'huddled masses' struck an almost discordant note. Already, the first barriers had been erected against the entry of undesirables."

Despite the growing body of anti-immigrant sentiment, initial efforts to limit the influx of newcomers were, for the most part, haphazard. Government was much smaller and more decentralized then, and no one could determine exactly who had legal jurisdiction over immigrants. So various court rulings virtually negated the restrictions imposed on both the federal and state level, and the flow of immigrants from Europe continued. In 1891, however, the Bureau of Immigration was created within the U.S. Treasury Department, and all responsibility for the regulation of immigration was consolidated under that federal bureau. Inspired by growing fears of mass immigration, the era of immigration restriction endorsed and enforced by the federal government was beginning to take shape in America.

During that period, the source of immigrants began to change. Instead of coming from Ireland, England and Germany, the immigrants were now coming from Italy, Austria-Hungary, Poland, Rumania, Portugal, Greece, Bulgaria and Russia. The Industrial Revolution and various political upheavals and military skirmishes had diminished the prospects for many of those countries' citizens and they, like the millions before them, decided that America was the place in which to find refuge, to start life anew.

A new wave of immigration to America developed, and between the turn of the century and 1914, 13 million people arrived on U.S. soil. The influx reached record levels in 1907, during which 1.28 million people moved to America. Italy eventually became the largest single source: between 1890 and 1914 nearly four million Italians immigrated to the United States.

The face in America's mirror was changing, and difficult times had arrived for America's highest-ranking politicians. The indigenous wage-working class of America resented and feared these newly arrived groups for economic reasons, but the industrialists who financed the politicians wanted the ever-increasing labor supply that the immigrants provided.

Various social conflicts were developing, as well. The Italian immigrants upset many white residents of

America's South, for example, because they had never learned in their native country to avoid associating with blacks.

The Germans who had immigrated to America were suspected by other Americans of still being loyal to the Kaiser, and the *Houston Post* editorialized in 1915 that "Germany seems to have lost all of her foreign possessions with the exception of Milwaukee, St. Louis and Cincinnati." (It is interesting to note that about 60 years later that emotion was adapted to create an anti-Cuban bumper sticker proclaiming: "Will the last American leaving Miami please bring the flag?")

Serious class conflicts were developing in America, the country whose founders had envisioned a place that would have no class system. In 1906 the conflicts between the various groups had grown so ugly that one Midwestern academic, Edwin A. Ross, publicly described the newly arriving immigrants as "the beaten members of beaten breeds."

Burying the Problem

The decades that have passed since that assessment was issued have, of course, mocked Ross's words. Those "beaten members of beaten breeds" helped make America so powerful, economically and militarily, that it could, if so inclined, have colonized the rest of the world—indeed, did colonize a number of smaller countries in a defacto way.

But in the early 1900s immigrant rivalries had grown so heated that Americans wanted to believe assertions such as those made by Ross, so President Theodore Roosevelt and other Republican leaders attempted to bury the smoldering controversy over immigration policy by proposing a long-term, full-scale investigation of the issue by the federal government. In February 1907 the Immigration Commission was formed.

It was made up of three senators, three members of the House of Representatives, and three outside "experts." Senator William Dillingham was its chairman, so it became known as the "Dillingham Commission."

Utilizing hundreds of staff members and more than one million dollars, the Dillingham Commission took three years to produce a hefty report. In the context of the past eight decades—in which the immigrant groups it investigated have produced innumerable successful leaders, scientists, entrepreneurs and intellectuals— the findings and recommendations of the commission seem at best laughable, although amazingly similar to those being tossed about today by proponents of increased immigration restrictions.

The new waves of immigrants that arrived between 1890 and 1911—such as the Italians—were "inferior," the Dillingham Commission found. The best course for America to take, the commission said, was one of slow growth that would allow immigrants to adapt to their new surroundings. That approach, the commission reported, would lessen the threat posed by immigrants to the employment opportunities of existing Americans.

The report was riddled with collections of "facts" that, if promulgated today, would be widely ridiculed and would most likely generate more than a few lawsuits. For example, it included a "Dictionary of Races" that attributed certain personal characteristics to various ethnic groups. Perhaps most ironically, it blamed immigration for retarding the development of trade unionism which, as the history of the union label demonstrates, was hardly the case.

Nevertheless, the Dillingham Commission's findings

were used as the basis for several pieces of legislation in subsequent years. However, none of them withstood the vetoes of President William Taft and, later, President Woodrow Wilson until the fear of America having to participate in World War I gave birth to an "Americanization" movement in 1915.

Soon after America was dragged into the war, the commission's findings were used to support passage of the Immigration Act of 1917. It was passed over the veto of President Wilson, and it required all immigrants over the age 16 to pass a literacy test. The act also effectively barred all Asian immigrants other than those from Japan, who were already being kept out under a previous "Gentleman's Agreement" between President Roosevelt and the Japanese government, and it made official for the first time the concept of nonimmigrant foreign workers, people who could come to America to work but who were barred from staying or ever becoming citizens.

It had taken nearly three *centuries* for the America of agrarian times to learn to fear and resent immigrants. But in less than three *decades* of rampant industrialization, the Land of Immigrants had evolved to the point where the formulation of complex and confusing legislation and international deals designed to keep immigrant labor out had become a major national endeavor.

A Vanishing Ideal

After the war ended in 1918, both Europe and America resumed their prewar drive toward industrialization. In Europe the process of industrialization was disrupting the economic lives of millions of people who had never known anything but agricultural or craftsmanship-based economies that were highly structured and regulated through such barriers to entry as guild systems, import restrictions and dissimilar languages and currencies.

In America, on the other hand, the Industrial Revolution was teaming up with an economy that was still relatively unstructured and with seemingly unlimited natural resources to create the largest and most dynamic mass market on earth. To many impoverished Europeans, things looked much better on the other side of the Atlantic, so the flow of European immigrants into America resumed once again.

At that point several factors began to work together to inspire new immigrant rivalries. Another depression hit the American economy in 1920–21, and the labor union movement was coming into full fury as the factories and other industrial installations grew larger and, in most cases, more dehumanizing. Partly in reaction to the depression, alternative economic structures such as communism began to be discussed, and immigrant intellectuals were frequently loudest among those doing the discussing. What's more, to the perennial American fear of Catholicism was added an unprecedentedly strong wave of anti-Semitism.

One of the leading instigators of anti-Semitism at that time was Henry Ford, founder of the Ford Motor Company. Seeking a group to blame for the depression of the early '20s and for a number of other things he felt were wrong about the American economy, Ford adopted a fanatical belief in concept of an international Jewish conspiracy whose goal it was to rule the world by disrupting the economic advancement of all other peoples. Utilizing the Dearborn *Independent*, a newspaper he owned, and a pamphlet entitled *The International Jews*, Ford vigorously spread his conspiracy theory.

From leading industrialists such as Ford as well as from members of earlier immigrant groups, American politicians were feeling great pressure to devise a means of limiting the entry of people from southern and eastern Europe—the troubling "new" immigration—while permitting entry of people from the countries that had sent most of the earlier immigrants who now constituted the largest part of the voting American public. So, in 1924 Congress enacted the Johnson-Reed Act, best known as the "National Origins Act." The act limited immigration from Europe to 150,000 persons per year, and allocated the quota for each country on the basis of the ethnic makeup of the U.S. population in 1890, more than three decades earlier. Without any real explanation, immigration from Japan was completely outlawed. This was America's first full-fledged immigration policy, and it was indisputably an attempt to institutionalize the status quo of America's ethnic and racial mix.

"With the enactment of this law an epoch in American history came to an end," observed Professor Jones in American Immigration. "After three centuries of free immigration, America all but completely shut her doors on newcomers. The Statue of Liberty would still stand in New York Harbor, but the verses on its base would henceforth be but a tribute to a vanished ideal."

Indeed, even Adolph Hitler was so favorably impressed by America's use of immigration restrictions to steer the evolution of the country's gene pool in favor of northwestern Europe—particularly in favor of Great Britain—that he wrote admiringly of America in his Nazi manifesto, Mein Kampf: "By simply excluding certain races from naturalization, it professes in slow beginning a view which is peculiar to the folkish state concept." A "folkish state" was, of course, what he had hoped to create in Germany.

The national origins system went into full effect in 1929, slowing immigration to America to a mere trickle. Meanwhile, the effects of World War I on Europe's stock of young men began to become manifest in a declining birth rate, which lessened the pressure to leave Europe in search of work. So when the depression of the 1930s, the one people in the late 20th century call "The Great Depression," began to cripple the American economy, immigration became a virtual non-issue.

As the '30s progressed and the Nazis gained power in Germany, however, a large number of German Jews were forced out of their country. Many of them wished to enter America, and some did, but many were refused. Those who did make it to America were met by numerous barriers designed to prevent them from earning a living in competition with depression-wracked Americans. And because influential American leaders such as Henry Ford had been so successful in spreading anti-Semitism, the newly arrived Jews frequently were accused of somehow being responsible for the depression.

One of the most dramatic exhibitions of America's fears of Jewish newcomers occurred in June 1939 when a ship named the SS St. Louis, carrying 930 Jews who had fled Hitler's rampage of terror in Germany, reached the coast of Florida. It was turned away by U.S. authorities and had to return to Europe, and many of its passengers subsequently died in concentration camps.

"If only they had let us in 50 years ago," a survivor of that incident told reporters during a 1989 ceremony memorializing the victims of the turnback. "It would have changed so many lives, it would have changed so many things."

To emphasize that 50th anniversary of what had become known as the "Voyage of the Damned," several Miami-based Jewish organizations staged a sinking off the Florida coast of a weather-beaten yacht that Hitler had ordered built, apparently for his own use.

"What a load off my shoulders to get rid of her," said J. J. Nelson, owner of the Florida shipyard where the controversial yacht had been stored for many years. Before deciding to donate the yacht to the Jewish groups, he had been approached by the American Nazi Party, which wanted to preserve the vessel. "People either wanted to spit on her or to worship her," Nelson added.

Another important shifting of humanity that occurred during the '30s was comprised of the victims of America's "dustbowl," a region of America's Great Plains that had been afflicted by dramatic shifting of soil cut loose from the earth by overly intensive farming. Hundreds of thousands of people abandoned their dust-filled and depression-stricken lives in the Great Plains and made their way to California which, because of its climate and the fertility of its soil, seemed to them to be the Promised Land.

The dustbowl "Okies" who made their way to the border of California often were turned away by police, even though they were merely moving *within* the "United" States. Those who managed to make it onto California soil were usually forced, like the people residing today along the Mexican side of America's Southwest border, to live in shanties, under bridges and in abandoned cars, trucks and buses. The Americans who first had made their way to California feared and resented the subsequent arrival of impoverished Americans who would have been happy to do California's dirty work in exchange for a regular roof over their heads.

War-Time Respite

When America entered World War II, immigration to America came to a virtual halt. America's war effort needed additional laborers badly, as evidenced by the "Rosie the Riveter" propaganda campaign that romanticized the entry of women into the wartime industrial workplace. But most people in Europe were too busy fighting for their own survival to think about moving. And after Japan's attack on Pearl Harbor, Asian-Americans were so feared by other Americans that even many of those who were born in America were rounded up and put into detention camps. What's more, transatlantic communications and transportation were either dedicated to military use or subject to interruption by acts of war.

The result was an acceleration of what historians call the "Great Migration," a long, slow movement of impoverished rural blacks from the American South to the North and Midwest. The labor shortages that developed in America's industrialized regions during World War I had encouraged some blacks to relocate, but when the European immigration resumed, the blacks were once again left with limited economic opportunities within the industrialization of America. The depression of the '30s stopped virtually all movement of human labor into and within America. But with the start of World War II, the Southern blacks once again became valuable labor to American manufacturing, and their delayed arrival as immigrants to America of the Industrial Era began to take place in earnest.

In the 1940s more than a million blacks migrated from the South to the heavily industrial northern regions of America. And, like the waves of immigrant labor that preceded them, they were met by resentment, fear and substandard living conditions.

As soon as the war was over and all the troops who had survived were brought home, however, industrial America became the desired destination for yet another group, those who had married American soldiers overseas and the children created via those marriages. In 1946 the United States enacted the "War Brides" and "Fiancées" acts, relaxing existing quotas to allow the soldiers' 150,000 wives and fiancées—and even a few husbands—and 25,000 children to enter from Europe. In 1947 similar legislation was passed to allow 5,000 Chinese and about 800 Japanese wives to immigrate to America.

These were all relatively small numbers, and pro-GI sentiment was still running high, so the arrival of these newcomers generated relatively little controversy.

The millions of other Europeans who had been displaced by the war were, however, another matter. Once again, America's tradition of immigrant rivalries sprang to life. But now the opponents of immigration began to incorporate jobilism into their positions. Congressmen from the Midwest and South, along with war-veteran groups and several organizations such as the John Birch Society that promoted hereditary patriotism, argued that to allow the entry of large numbers of displaced persons would endanger the jobs and housing opportunities of GIs, while exposing the country to a wave of communist subversives.

Eventually, however, humanitarianism won out to a degree and the Displaced Persons Act of 1948, which was subsequently amended in 1950, allowed about 400,000 victims of the war to enter the United States over a four-year period. A fourth of that special quota was set aside to accommodate people of German origin who had been residing in the Baltic States, along with war orphans and people stranded in the Far East by the war.

In 1953 a similar law, the Refugee Relief Act, was passed to deal with the wave of people fleeing from communist countries and from West Germany and Italy, both of which were having a difficult time recovering from the war. Under that law, 214,000 people entered America during a period of slightly less than four years.

America's resistance to immigrants remained so strong, however, that politicians had to make compromises that would accommodate both humanitarian urges and the conflicting immigration-related fears. Consequently, the people who entered under the special postwar refugee laws were charged against their homelands' regular prewar immigration quotas. Thus, the rate of immigration from those countries ballooned temporarily but was ostensibly severely restricted long into the future.

The Fighting Continues

Despite the affluence that America enjoyed for nearly four decades following World War II, its tradition of immigrant rivalries has never abated. As the American economic scene has become more structured and regulated, however, the rivalries have tended to become more sophisticated and complex. Earlier confrontations usually took place primarily between the immigrant groups at the bottom of the economic ladder and would-be newcomers who seemed to threaten the meager status of those already on shore. Now, however, the opposition is often made up of those at the highest end of America's income range.

For example, in 1989 a major political and public relations conflict broke out between about 400 physicians who had relocated to Miami from embattled Nicaragua and the American medical establishment. The Nicaraguan doctors, many of whom had been forced down into such things as janitorial jobs, argued that the medical training in their homeland had been roughly equal to that in America and that they should, consequently, be issued Florida medical licenses. There also was a humanitarian aspect to their desires, they argued, because most of the 150,000 Nicaraguan refugees in Florida were poor and couldn't afford to avail themselves of America's increasingly expensive healthcare system.

As part of their efforts to keep the Nicaraguans from practicing medicine in America, the U.S. physicians had set up a special licensing test, in English, that was administered only to physicians educated at foreign medical schools. It was much more rigorous than that administered to physicians trained in America, and even those who passed it still were required to spend a year as a resident in an American hospital, and then take another federal licensing test.

Florida State Senator Ilena Ros-Lehtinen of Miami, who sponsored legislation that would help the Nicaraguan physicians obtain American licenses, told the news media that the American medical groups were afraid that the Nicaraguans would cut in on their profits.

"More and more Central American professionals are going to be coming to this country," she noted. "If these professional organizations and regulatory boards keep a hard-nosed attitude and do not allow people to practice their professions, they're going to deny medical help to the very people they want to serve. And they're going to deny the immigrant community role models who inspire others to become professionals."

The physicians' clash demonstrates that immigrant rivalries are still very much a part of America's economic system. And the post-World War II period added still another form of human rivalry to the American landscape. It was a rivalry between people who saw capitalism as the best economic system on earth, and those who saw capitalism as the enemy of mankind. America's belief in private property and private enterprise clashed in the wake of the war with the belief of Russians, Chinese and other peoples in the economic concept of community ownership and cooperative work, "communism."

The "Cold War" between those conflicting value systems began to escalate just a few years after the end of World War II, and America's fear of immigrants took on a strange new complexion.

CHAPTER 3

McCarran and McCarthy: Drafting Immigrants for the Cold War

I N CONTEMPORARY AMERICA communism is not something one discusses in polite company, other than to
observe that it failed to fulfill many of its promises to
the people of Russia and China. Communism is an
emotion-filled concept that, like religion and the Mafia,
is considered detrimental to comfortable social inter-
course.

But in depression-wracked America of the 1930s, the
option of communism was being discussed energetically in many circles as a possible alternative to the
industrial capitalism system that seemed to have left so
many millions of Americans down—that had turned
many of them into homeless drifters who roamed the

country in desperation, searching for a way to earn a living.

It was within that context, ironically, that legendary folk musician Woodrow Wilson "Woody" Guthrie composed the song that many contemporary Americans consider to be the country's rightful national anthem, "This Land Is Your Land." But just as America has romanticized the circumstances surrounding the writing and dedication of the poem that adorns the base of the Statue of Liberty, the stressful origins of Guthrie's most famous and loved song have been sterilized in the American culture that has evolved since World War II.

In his highly regarded biography *Woody Guthrie: A Life* (Alfred A. Knopf, 1980), author Joe Klein points out that Guthrie had been traveling about in America during the '30s and had witnessed, firsthand, hardships and inequities created by the cruelties of nature and the American industrial economy. Using railroad boxcars as his primary means of transportation, Guthrie observed bankers, politicians, lawyers and industrialists—those who had instituted and benefited most from the rules by which America's farming and wage-working masses lived—prospering, while many factory workers, farmers and their families scrounged for scraps of food.

In response, Guthrie sang about the hundreds of thousands of people whom he had seen "stranded on that road that goes from sea to sea," of farm sweat-laborers from Mexico who became known only by the dehumanized label of "deportees," and of smiling bankers who used a fountain pen, not a gun, to rob people of their homes and farms. He even adapted an old Christian hymn, "This World Is Not My Home," into a mournful song about victims of the Great Plains "dustbowl" who had "no home in this world any-more."

Along the way, Guthrie became sympathetic to the communist movement in America—a movement that had smoldered in obscurity for decades but burst into political flames during the depression—and he some-times wrote and performed songs for communist politi-cal rallies. Although his motivations apparently were humanistic, not political, he frequently was castigated and snubbed by established society because of his anti-establishment political sympathies.

However, the one aspect of American culture that irritated Guthrie most consistently was not the domi-nance of industrial capitalism but the ability of the dominant cliques in America to cover up their mis-takes—and their abuses of the American economic sys-tem—through their influence on the mass media.

During the Great Depression, the industrial estab-lishment's constant whipping of the issue of jobs for its own political gain had left deep intellectual and emo-tional scars on the American rank-and-file. By early 1939, for example, jobilism had become so dominant that a legislative proposal to allow 20,000 German chil-dren who were refugees of the Nazi terror to enter America was allowed to become law only after political leaders assured the American public that, because of the range of their ages, no more than 2,500 of those children would enter the American job market in any one year as they reached adulthood.

Job-shocked America had sunk to the point where it feared even those homeless chidlren, and Guthrie didn't like to see people dealing with one another in that way. What's more, in the winter of 1940 he became particularly infuriated by the fact that wherever he traveled, whenever he turned on the radio, he inevitably heard the late Irving Berlin's cute-and-gushing "God Bless America," which he considered to be virtual propaganda distributed on behalf of the establishment.

So after wandering into New York City and staying a night as a houseguest of fellow folksinger Burl Ives, Guthrie checked into a fleabag hotel on Sixth Avenue, and then decided to vent the frustration generated in him by "God Bless America" by setting the record straight through music. He began writing a protest parody called "God Blessed America," which had at the end of each verse a tag line: "God blessed America for me." The emphasis was on the words "for me."

To rebut Berlin's propaganda, Guthrie created a song that showcased some of the key arguments that were being made by those who favored the institution of communism or other anti-capitalist systems in America: the contradiction between the natural abundance of America and the specter of hungry people standing in relief lines, and the moral infractions that can be generated by abuse of the concept of private property.

Guthrie often took years to polish a song into a form that accurately expressed his thoughts, and "God Blessed America" was one of those songs. By the time he finally sat down to record it about five years later, he had changed the tag line to "This land was made for you and me." In the process of refinement, the messages the song contained had become even more poignant and defiant.

Despite the fact that it was first recorded by a little-known recording team that specialized in the then-new genre of American folk music, the song grew slowly but consistently in popularity. Today, it is known by the title "This Land Is Your Land" and is revered around the world. But in the process of commercialization, it has been sterilized to the point where Woody's son, Arlo, sings at least one of the defiant verses (usually the one that mocks signs designating the boundaries of private real estate) at each of his concerts to fulfill a pact he made with his father before Woody's death.

The existence of that pact with Arlo indicates that Woody somehow knew postwar America would want to forget about the human suffering that inspired "This Land Is Your Land." By the time he recorded it, World War II had put America back to work. When the GIs returned triumphant, America's attention turned to the process of household creation: getting married, having babies, building houses, buying cars and furniture, planting lawns.

With the rest of the industrialized world facing several decades of postwar reconstruction, America was on top, and the economic tide began to rise for nearly every American. The breadlines, the hobos, the "Okies" and the foreclosure-hungry bankers of the depression days about which Guthrie had written so many songs had all but disappeared. With the postwar baby boom, America was unwittingly creating it first homegrown labor force and mass consumer market to fuel its postwar economic euphoria. Because of all that activity, material wealth was beginning to overflow the cup and cascade down to Americans for whom the future had seemed so bleak in the decade just before the war.

Meanwhile, communism—archenemy of the concept of private property—was evolving as the postwar economic system of many of the largest countries on earth. But communism was at the same time becoming the worst of all villains to working-class Americans— tens of millions of whom were amassing substantial quantities of private material wealth for the first time in their personal and family histories.

For the first time in its history, America had reached a point where it might have stopped squabbling over economic opportunities, when it might have laid to rest all its immigrant rivalries and begun considering the matter of immigration scientifically instead of emotionally. With its factories pounding around the clock and their smokestacks belching up into the skies, America might have purged itself of the rotting residue of the Great Depression by throwing its doors open to all who wanted to enter and work their way up within the citadel of free enterprise.

Millions of people from around the war-scarred world wanted to leave the decimation of their homelands and the regimentation of communism behind in those days. They wanted to relocate their lives to the victorious Land of the Free, Home of the Brave, and to join in the celebration of America's global military dominance and developing economic superiority.

With its belly full, America could have become suddenly generous in its attitudes toward immigrants. It could have pushed its golden door open wide, casting aside the fears and resentments born of the dark early days of the Industrial Revolution and the equally traumatic depression of the '30s. But as Woody Guthrie seems to have anticipated, that's not the way that America reacted.

Some political operatives began to see opportunities in the exploitation of America's historic wave of patriotism, its newly accumulating material wealth and the resultant newly aroused fears of the extremely militant communist fervor that was sweeping other countries. The newspapers, the newsreels and even the newly available technology of television all displayed before Americans the sparseness and regimentation of communist countries, and the newly comfortable Americans didn't like what they saw.

The stage was set for a huge emotional outpouring of patriotic spirit in America. Communism had become the common enemy upon which Americans could focus their postwar enthusiasm. But then, a unique cast of players, operating within an equally unique set of circumstances, got U. S. immigration policy all tangled up in the "Red Scare."

Fighting in McCarthy's Shadow

The late Senator Joseph McCarthy, a Republican from Wisconsin is, of course, the person most commonly associated with America's communist fears of the late '40s and early '50s. Assisted, perhaps incited, by several very ambitious staff members who were particularly adept at manipulating the news media, McCarthy raised himself up onto a pedestal of righteousness as the fearless defender of the American Way and archenemy of communism—leaving in his wake the wrecked lives of many of the people he wrongly and haphazardly accused of subversion.

Indeed, the process of exciting and encouraging fears of communism for political gain is now listed in dictionaries and encyclopedias under "McCarthyism," and some people still argue that it was "Tail Gunner Joe" McCarthy who saved America from a clandestine communist plot to eradicate the American way of life from the face of the globe.

But, in fact, there were two other people in power in Washington at that time who fought harder—and, by all indications, much more sincerely—against the spread of communism: the late Patrick A. McCarran, a Democrat who served as a U. S. senator from Nevada from 1933 until his death in 1954, and Eva B. Adams, McCarran's administrative assistant and confidant from 1940 until his death.

Together, McCarran and Adams shaped and championed the legislation, enacted on Christmas Eve 1952, and known as the "McCarran-Walter Act," that became the keystone of America's immigration policies during the immediate postwar decades and at this writing remains the framework for American immigration law. The process by which they accomplished that historic task became tangled, however, in the manipulations and stressed emotions of the McCarthy Era. The evolution of the legislation was, therefore, amazingly emotional and unscientific, particularly in light of the millions of lives that have been affected, and will be affected, by that which the team of McCarran and Adams wrought.

Like every other attempt to regulate immigration to America, the McCarran-Walter Act (officially, the Immigration and Nationality Act of 1952) became law with no scientific consideration of how many immigrants America needed.

The Team from Reno

When I met Adams in 1989 she was about 81 years old and residing in a modest home in a suburb-like neighborhood of Reno, Nevada. She had never married. Well dressed and well groomed, she appeared to be a gracefully aging sorority girl who had never lost her practiced social bearing. She looked much younger than her actual years. The only outward indication of the importance of the home's principal occupant in

American history was a luxury sedan bearing the vanity license plate "Eva 1" parked in the driveway.

In the early '50s, America's news media apparently became so enthralled with McCarthy's headline-grabbing stunts that they forgot to follow the immigration-related work of McCarran and his spunky colleague Adams in any detail. Indeed, even in Nevada where the largest airport, major thoroughfares and many other things are named "McCarran," many people don't know the international significance of their former home-state senator, and even fewer have ever heard of his loyal sidekick. Consequently, the telling details of how America set its postwar immigration policies reside only in memories of Adams and the senator's immediate family, and in several document collections that have been donated to libraries.

Yet in the immigration-conscious early '50s, *The Washington Post* described McCarran as the most powerful person in Congress; Adams, to whom he delegated much of his power and on whom he relied for guidance, was by all indications a close second.

Washington has long been a city where the best restaurants are filled with what a Washington-weary fellow journalist once described to me as "old men and their nieces"; as Washington insiders know too well, those poised and attractive young women often wield as much power as the officially powerful older men with whom they dine. In the days before women entered national politics in significant numbers as candidates for office, this was particularly true: A sophisticated, educated woman's surest route to international power in America often was service as a loyal, low-profile understudy to a male member of Congress.

Adams was no exception to that syndrome. Her records and recollections of those years—and the records and recollections of others familiar with the evolution of the McCarran-Walter Act—leave no doubt that Adams is the last living member of a small political clique that made the "Cold War" against communism an American institution for nearly four decades and, with the same pass of the wand of governmental power, established the standards by which America would control immigration through its post-World War II boom times and beyond.

Adams is an extremely bright and witty person who punctuates her conversation with restrained chuckles. Her laughter is not the nervous kind that relieves stress, but rather the comfortable, wizened kind that comes with the luxury of being able to look at the complexities and contradictions of life in a rear-view mirror. Her extremely ambitious, quietly orchestrated approach to politics is best captured by a personal philosophical statement included in her listing in *Who's Who in America:*

> With all the competition in this world, any person, male or female, must be willing to do one thing to succeed—and this is WORK HARD. I have never felt the long arm of discrimination because I was a woman sometimes in a man's job. I feel this is true because I knew when I took any such job, that I had to "work like a man," while retaining my femininity, but never "overusing" it.

Despite the fact that Senator McCarran has been dead for more than three decades, Adams still delights in talking about the relationship she and he shared. Her eyes light up when she talks about the man she typically refers to simply as "the senator." She laughingly volunteers the fact that some people—McCarthy's henchmen, she still suspects—used her closeness to McCarran maliciously to depict her as the senator's mistress.

"I've never smoked in my life, but they said that I visited Senator McCarran in a room in a town between here and Washington, and that the place was full of cigarettes with lipstick on them. Now, that alone should have exonerated me because I didn't know how to smoke," she told me during a conversation in the living room of her home.

During the '30s and '40s, she explained, America's immigration laws and regulations had become a jumble of exceptions, contradictions and accommodations of special interests. Logic, economic or otherwise, was nowhere to be found.

"If you could understand that law, you're a better man than I am," she quipped. "It was literally a con-glomeration of little things. The first thing we did was—I can still remember the fellows working on it—was to take scissors to copies of the (old) law and put material under the relevant heading, where it belonged.

"This was an unsought task. They had been putting it off so long, they couldn't put it off any longer. The people in charge of immigration were just over-whelmed with uncertainties."

Shepherd to Senator

The story of how such an unsought-but-monumental task ended up on the desk of Senator Patrick Anthony McCarran is an unusual one, the climax of which can seem either tragic or profoundly just, depending on one's point of view.

Born in 1876 in Reno, he was the only child of

immigrants from Ireland who, unlike most of their countrymen, ventured out past the industrial ghettos of America's East Coast and into the wide-open spaces of the American West. His father had arrived in Nevada as a soldier, and after the Civil War homesteaded a ranch along a river just east of Reno. His mother had worked her way west as a domestic servant, and met and married her husband in Reno. Consequently, the senator's parents became atypical Irish-American immigrants. They were landholders and agricultural business owners in a wide-open part of the American West, not industrial wage-workers crammed into towns that circled the factories and mills of the Northeast.

Patrick's formal education started at age 10 in a one-room school house. Later, as student at Reno High School and at the University of Nevada, Patrick was an academic stand-out—although, because of his late start in school, he was about four years older than most of his classmates. But when his father was seriously injured in an accident, Patrick had to return to the family ranch to tend to the sheep herd that was the family business. Consequently, he spent little time in the company of any people other than his parents.

In the tradition of the dominant Irish matriarch, his mother repeatedly urged her son to run for the Nevada Assembly. He did, and was elected in 1903, and subsequently added an independent study of law to his sheepherding and governmental duties. In those days, one didn't need a college degree in law to be an attorney, so in 1905, the future senator took the bar exam and became Atty. Patrick A. McCarran.

After being admitted to the practice of law, McCarran affiliated with a small Reno law firm where, by all accounts, his rural upbringing merged with his self-taught knowledge of the law and the rugged individualist attitudes of his parents and the still-young American West to give him what in contemporary America would be described as a "conservative" or "right wing" orientation. In attorney McCarran's mind, the U. S. Constitution could never bow to special interests; America was governed by laws, not men, and a law was a law until the legislative body designated by the U. S. Constitution changed it.

The Art of Kissing Babies

In the decades that followed, McCarran became adept at local politics. Nevada was a very sparsely populated state—more like a small town or a big-city ward than a state, from a political science perspective—where politicians met, at one time or another, virtually all of their constituents. McCarran was the classic Irish-American politician, raised with the simple but colorful values and mannerisms of the Irish countryside, who could easily win votes in Nevada of those times. He was a kisser of babies and an eloquent ceremonial speaker who knew how to use the political spoils system to buy the allegiance of working-class famlies, and the power of government to win the support of Nevada's business leaders.

Candidate McCarran was a man's man who became the subject of barstool legends by doing such things as sharing a drink with rough-and-tumble union leaders and volunteering his legal expertise in defense of the girls who worked in Nevada's brothels.

McCarran's hometown of Reno was a place of simple, rugged tastes and concerns, a place far removed—geographically, economically, and intellectually—from most of the stresses of America's coasts, where so many industrial-era immigrants were piling in and piling up.

It was during his youth in Reno and surrounding towns, apparently, that McCarran began to develop his viewpoint of what kind of person was the "right" kind of person to be an American—the viewpoint that he carried with him to Washington, D. C., in 1933 after he was elected to the U. S. Senate at age 56.

"He had nothing but respect for immigration and immigrants, because his father had come as a stowaway at age 14, his family having starved, and his mother came over in steerage," said Sister Margaret P. McCarran, a retired Roman Catholic nun and the senator's eldest child, when we talked in 1989 on the same McCarran ranch that her immigrant grandfather had homesteaded in the 19th century.

Sister Margaret's diminutive size, fine features and affable nature belie her intellectual complexity and fervor. She was, by all accounts, the family member closest to the senator intellectually. She still resides on and runs the huge family ranch, which is located just one interstate highway exit east of the notorious but still legal Mustang Ranch brothel.

Senator McCarran had, she pointed out, gone through some traumatic experiences because of early clashes between communism and capitalism in America. In particular, Sister Margaret recalls, he seemed to have been upset by the oddity of a socialist enclave that had been established not far from his family's ranch around the turn of the century, and by violence that had been instigated by the Industrial Workers of the World among workers in the isolated Nevada silver mining town of Tonapah, where her father had served a stint as district attorney shortly after entering the legal profession and politics.

"He was, naturally, afraid of anything that was as

unlawful as that," Sister Margaret said. "As for the needs and pursuits of labor, he was far from being against them. The railroad brotherhood always loved him, in spite of the fact that his father and mother didn't like the railroad for what it had done to the ranch—the way it had gone through it and its high-handedness. But he was against the infiltration of socialist and communist ideas. He didn't want to see the American labor movement destroyed from the inside."

Sophisticated Women

Sister Margaret doesn't view herself as having encouraged her father's campaign against communism, but her professional history indicates a high probability that she did.

Born in 1904 in Reno about four years before Eva Adams, Sister Margaret became interested early in her academic career in the Fabian Society, a socialist group founded in London during the nineteenth century which reached its peak of popularity in the 1940s. The Fabians stressed the superiority of education and intellect over other forms of power in creating a more humane world through socialist policies, and for a time that concept was appealing to the religious and humanistic Sister Margaret.

But as her studies continued, she recalls, she began to discover what she felt were dangerous errors in the Fabian philosophy, as well as in the somewhat related communistic approach to economic and political life. In her role as an associate professor of history and political science at Holy Names College in Oakland, California, Sister Margaret became a leading debunker of Fabian and communist philosophy. She wrote several books on Fabianism—including one which, she says, her religious order forbade her to submit for publication because of its controversial nature.

"At the college, they say 'Sister Margaret sees a communist under every bed,'" she told me with a defiant laugh and a shrug. "And I say 'No, I see *two* communists under every bed.'"

It was such fears of communism, not hatred of immigrants, that inspired her father, she says. With obvious fondness and pride, she recounts an incident involving immigrants that occurred when her senator-father came to visit her on the campus of Holy Names College. Several Filipino men who worked in the college kitchen had heard of his impending visit and, recalling his support of earlier special legislation that allowed them to enter America, the men dressed up in their military uniforms and formed an impromptu honor guard as Senator McCarran walked through the cafeteria.

Certainly Senator McCarran and his eldest daughter couldn't have helped but share philosophies during their times together. The senator also couldn't help but have been influenced by the equally intellectual but more wordly Adams. She was about 32 years younger than he, had had an early education that was much more conventional than his, and had graduated from the University of Nevada in 1928. She taught for a few years in Southern Nevada, then went to Columbia University in Manhattan, where she received a master's degree in English in 1936.

Columbia was at that time a center of varied, often "radical" political and economic thought. Adams, then in her late 20s, applied for and was granted admission to International House, a special dormitory for students from a wide variety of countries which, consequently.

housed a very cosmopolitan group. To this young smalltown schoolteacher from the West, New York City in the '30s was an amazingly unruly yet exciting place.

"I don't know where I got this idea about living at International House, but somewhere I had heard of it and felt that that was where I wanted to live," she told an interviewer at the University of Nevada years later during the creation of an oral history. "But when I arrived there, the cab strike—and people said take the subway. Me and my sixteen pieces of luggage. But kid-like, I carried everything with me, and I tell you this was a traumatic experience because I didn't know what to do.

"Finally, I found a nice old porter who got me into a scab cab, and we drove up to International House. They threw rocks at that taxi; a group came out on one occasion, and tried to turn it over. Ohhhh, what an introduction to any city. It was really weird."

Nevertheless, International House turned out to be the intense intellectual experience Adams had hoped for, and then some.

"But my year at International House was most gratifying because of the people I met—people from all over the world," she said in her oral history. "And I learned to play bridge. I was taught by a Chinese man and an Arab and a Jewish man. The combination meant nothing to me at all. It was just part of life to me—if anybody ever told me then of the struggles that would have ensued through the years, I couldn't have believed them."

Indeed, how could she have known that one of the friends she made during those free-thinking days at Columbia, Burl Ives, would several years later have to ask her to rescue him from a dark drama in which both he and she would be principal players? How could this back-country woman on an intellectual lark in the big city have known that Ives would, just a few years later, provide shelter and companionship to such odd and disruptive people as Woody Guthrie?

The Team Is Formed

After completing her studies at Columbia, Adams returned to Reno and joined the faculty of the University of Nevada. She and her family were active in local political, business and social circles—which, in Reno, were really all one big circle—so she and McCarran became acquainted. In 1940 the senator asked her to move to Washington to join his office staff, and she accepted. She subsequently became his administrative assistant and confidant, the woman behind the man. Assuming even the senator's health as her personal responsibility, Adams would write to Sister Margaret periodically to keep her advised of the senator's physical status and emotional disposition.

Ever the student, Adams spent her free time studying law. Eventually, she added to her previous liberal arts degrees a bachelor's degree in law from American University and a master's degree in law from George Washington University. In 1950 she was admitted to the practice of law in Nevada and Washington, D. C. Professionally, she had become at least the senator's equal.

Things progressed relatively smoothly for the team of McCarran and Adams until several years after the war. While America was beginning its postwar climb to world economic dominance, people in many other parts of the world were suffering in the wake of the war. Many of those suffering were relatives of people who had immigrated to America before the war. Others were people with whom American military men—and in a few cases women—had fallen in love, might have had children, and in some cases married while serving overseas. The result was a huge growth in demand for changes in immigration restrictions to allow all these people to enter postwar America.

At the end of the war, President Harry S. Truman issued a directive admitting 40,000 war refugees to America. In 1946 Congress enacted the War Brides Act that allowed in an extra 120,000 persons. In 1948 the Displaced Persons Act was passed, allowing in more than 400,000 persons ahead of schedule, as measured by the quotas then in existence. But public pressure for more relaxation of the immigration laws continued to build.

In 1949, McCarran became chairman of the Senate Judiciary Committee, which was responsible for such things as immigration law, by virtue of his political status. Suddenly, the country lawyer and small-town politican found himself the focal point of a huge and sometimes vicious global controversy. Immigration law, America's perennial political hot potato, had been dropped into his lap.

"Immigration was becoming a problem from three viewpoints," Adams recalled in her oral history. "Not only the mass of applications for admission to this country. Second, the complete confusion of the immigration laws. They had been amended and re-amended, and amendments to amendments, to the point where you couldn't find what the law was. And third, there was a great feeling that the immigration laws were abused for the purpose of getting communists into the country."

It was in that atmosphere that McCarran, now suffering from recurrent heart and stomach troubles, became a victim of circumstance, Adams argues.

"The senator wasn't interested in keeping Jewish people out, or certainly not Italians, or any of the others," she told me, alluding to various accusations that were made during that period. "It [immigration policy] became a controversy when it got mixed up with the Displaced Persons Act.

"The people who ran the processing centers for those [displaced] people became disturbed because, evidently, there was a certain type of person—crusader types—and some of them were out-and-out communists. And some of the people in the displaced persons camps felt that some of these people were not truly displaced people. They were plants and individuals who were anxious to work for the cause of communism in this country.

"The communist thing became almost a violent thing during that period. There were accidents in airplane plants and so forth and I don't know if it was the press or who it was that was attributing them to communist infiltration. Well, now, that was never proved, and I'm inclined not to believe it, but it was a curious predicament and it just got real sticky," she said.

To combat what he perceived as a serious threat from communism to the continued existence of the United States, McCarran authored the Internal Security Act, which was enacted in 1950. That act generally strengthened the power of the federal government to exclude or deport persons who were suspected of being alien subversives. And suspected subversion was, of course, the stuff of which McCarthy's mud-slinging campaign against communism was made.

"Unfortunately, this was the era when Joe McCarthy

was talking the loudest and being the most vehement. He did his darnedest to get Senator McCarran's backing, and so forth, and the senator wouldn't do it," Adams told me. "People went so far as to talk about going to war over this. I'm a peaceful soul, but I was in the middle of it."

The behind-the-scenes tension between McCarran and McCarthy became so great, Adams believes, that McCarthy's staff began looking for ways to blackmail McCarran into an unequivocal political alliance with McCarthy. They used such methods, she believes, as planting rumors that she was the senator's mistress. Adams admits, nevertheless, that despite his refusal to become directly involved in McCarthy's anti-communist activities, McCarran had the power to call off McCarthy's barking dogs. The case of her friend Burl Ives is an example of that. Because of his association with such people as Guthrie and Guthrie's sidekick-protege Pete Seeger, Ives became a target of McCarthy's hunt for communist sympathizers in the entertainment industry.

"Burl Ives has been a friend of mine for years. We went to Columbia together at one point," Adams recalled in her oral history. "He was accused by somebody of being inclined toward communism. He called me, and I told the senator he had called, and I said 'Can't we do anything to clear his record?'

"He (McCarran) said, 'Surely.' He said, 'If we're going to determine that they are communists, we should have the authority to determine that they aren't.' So he said, 'Have him come down and we'll have a hearing.' And we cleared him completely, which I thought was great. That was an aspect few people know. But he did that in many cases. We'd have a hearing, and the decision of the committee was that so-and-so was not engaged in subversive activities, which meant a great deal to a lot of them, believe me."

McCarthy's greatest shortcoming, Adams contends, was not his pursuit of communists in government, but the people with whom he surrounded himself.

"Senator McCarthy was a fine person and a good friend, and had contributed much in the Senate," she told me. "But he had the propensity for hiring the darnedest people you ever saw. They weren't the type of people who should have been in government, who should have been doing the reporting, because I'm sure their reports didn't always follow their investigations. . . . His staff was weird.

"Senator McCarran thought of McCarthy as a very able person, and he admired his willingness to fight against communism. But he also used to tell me that McCarthy was like a wild horse with no reins," she said.

"Then, to add fuel to the fire, the editor of a paper in Las Vegas, (the late Hank Greenspun of the Las Vegas Sun)—who just hated Senator McCarran, and I never knew why, and I at that point had never met him—just harangued and harangued. But he was a good writer and a good newspaperman, and his stuff got picked up all over the country. So the thing just accumulated until everyone accused the senator of persecuting the displaced persons, of persecuting the Jewish people—which was as far wrong as it could be—and I forget which other nationalities it was that he was supposedly trying to keep out," she said.

"He didn't have any particular interest in keeping out people who made good citizens, who weren't coming over here for an ulterior motive, and who fit into all

the ramification of the immigration law. It was circum-
stantial, but that's what history is."

Sharing the Heat

During the McCarthy era few people believed that
the powerful senator from Nevada was merely a victim
of circumstance. McCarran began to share the enmity
that many Americans felt toward McCarthy and his
tactics. To win elections in the '40s, McCarran and his
supporters had sometimes convinced his largely paro-
chial home-state constituents that his opponents were
financed by "New York" money, which was interpreted
by some to be a euphemism for "Jewish money," so
McCarran was sometimes accused of anti-Semitism.
That accusation also gained credence from the fact that
many of the people who wanted to immigrate to America from behind the "Iron Curtain" at that time, and
whom McCarran therefore suspected of being communist infiltrators, were Jews.

What's more, some supporters of increased immigration limits for persons from predominantly Catholic
countries didn't like McCarran's resistance to such increases, so he was sometimes accused of being anti-
Catholic, an odd label for an Irish-Catholic man with
two daughters who became nuns. McCarran's predicament was made worse by the fact that, by the early '50s
he had reached the pinnacle of his political power and
became a natural focal point for public criticism.

"It was also the period when [McCarran] became the
butt of some of Herbert Block's [Herblock's] most cruel
cartoons in *The Washington Post*, depicting him as fat,
slovenly and unshaven, a precursor of Herblock's later,
famous, unshaven McCarthy and Nixon," notes Jerome

E. Edwards, a professor of history at the University of
Nevada, Reno, in his book *Pat McCarran: Political Boss
of Nevada* (University of Nevada Press, 1982).

McCarran had never felt the need to answer to the
national news media, and his constituency really
didn't much care what he did concerning the primarily
East Coast controversy over immigration. All the voters
in Nevada wanted from McCarran were small-time personal favors from a powerful politician in Washington,
Edwards points out. So McCarran simply dug in his
heels on the immigration front, allowing Adams to run
interference with fellow political leaders and to fend
off journalists that she felt were hostile, while he stayed
his determined course toward a victory for constitutional law and against communist subversion.

McCarran wanted America's immigration regulations
to be codified in a fashion that would fit with his belief
in the sanctity of the law, and he wanted to protect
America from communism and what he called "con-
quest by immigration." He wanted America to be a
place primarily for good Americans, whom he appears
to have defined roughly as being people who resembled
his parents. And he had the power, determination and
political arrogance to try to bring all those things about.

The husky, homespun Irish-American shepherd from
Nevada chose to defend his position by punching it out
with the very worldly and sophisticated intellects on
the East Coast, and he soon found himself up against a
wall with his critics' hands around his throat. Nationally and even internationally, McCarran became the
object of such venom that he began to get substantial
amounts of hate mail, to which he sometimes responded by having Adams use federal agencies to in-
vestigate the writers.

Despite his own humble immigrant roots, he had

become the most despised person in all of America's long history of immigration controversies. Even a constituent from his home state who had the same last name as the senator wrote McCarran a letter that called him "the pot-bellied Hitler of the desert."

Representative Francis E. Walter, a Democrat from eastern Pennsylvania who had been thrown into the fray by virtue of being chairman of the House Judiciary Subcommittee on Immigration Affairs, never exhibited the fervor that McCarran did for the issues of communism and immigration policy. Known primarily as a pork-barrel politician most interested in passing bills that would benefit the voters of the factory and mining communities he represented, Walter was nearly twenty years younger than McCarran and lacked the senator's clout. He had been teamed with McCarran, however, by the conservative faction of the Democratic party that opposed President Franklin D. Roosevelt's liberal New Deal policies, and he was depicted in the early postwar years as a communism fighter by Democratic party leaders anxious to counterbalance the popularity of the Republican McCarthy.

Walter would send over to McCarran various proposals for immigration law amendments intended to please special interests who had appealed to Democratic house members, and the senator would reject most of them, Adams recalls. (She also recalls, as an aside, that Walter "hated Italians.")

A Forgotten Ideal

At no point, Adams told me, were the needs of the American workforce or any other economic factors discussed during formulation of the McCarran-Walter Act. It appears, however, that McCarran had envisioned an immigration policy more sophisticated than that which he eventually decided so firmly to enact.

According to an oral history created by Norman Biltz—a Nevada businessman, political wheeler-dealer and reputedly the closest male friend McCarran ever had—the senator envisioned and often discussed with Biltz a system that would allow American immigration flows to be matched to workforce needs. But the urge to protect America against communist takeover became so overwhelming to McCarran—"This was the thing that he worked on and dreamed of night and day, to block every possible way," Biltz said—that the senator never took the time to separate and refine the two issues.

Consequently, when the McCarran-Walter Act became law, it was little more than the codification of the old laws that the senator had set out to achieve, heavily peppered with new clauses aimed at communist subversives. (Some brief descriptions of the act in encyclopedias and similar publications suffer from over-simplification in that they say the act opened the way for immigration from Asia. In fact, the act contained only token new openings for Asians. Those increases, the senator's files indicate, were intended by McCarran to dissuade people of such countries as Korea from becoming increasingly anti-American and, consequently, pro-communist.)

Despite all the controversy, America's immigration laws remained a collection of petty interests with roots in the nineteenth century that continued to tilt the ethnic mix of America toward northwestern Europe. The rules had been made more orderly, to be sure, and some long-term injustices such as the inability of Asians to become U. S. citizens were corrected, but the opportunity to make the immigration laws *logical* had been swamped by the clamor over communism. The progeny of immigrant rivalries of the '20s and '30s had become the law of the land for America's postwar era. To fight communism, McCarran, McCarthy and Adams had drafted immigrants into their Cold War army.

"We didn't change the law, we codified it," Adams told me. "It was a misunderstood thing. I don't think the public ever knew what our mission was."

In September 1954, less than two years after the passage of the McCarran-Walter Act, McCarran dropped dead after delivering a political speech in Hawthorne, Nevada. Adams flew back to Reno from Washington to direct the funeral arrangements.

A Lone Survivor

At the same time, McCarthy's popularity was evaporating. He eventually was publicly discredited, and in 1957 died of liver disease and excessive alcohol consumption. Nevertheless, a group meets each year in his hometown of Appleton, Wisconsin, to publicly reiterate their belief that "Tail Gunner Joe" was right.

Walter's political fortunes waned with the McCarthy era as well, although he kept his name in print by fighting to preserve the basic concepts of the McCarran-Walter Act during the Eisenhower and Kennedy administrations. In May 1963, after losing the relatively high profile he had enjoyed because of his nominal role in the setting of immigration policy, he died in Washington of leukemia.

Adams was the only long-term survivor of the front lines of the first battles of the Cold War. She went on to serve as administrative assistant to two subsequent senators from Nevada, Ernest Brown and Alan Bible. She further solidified her political status during that period by conducting a school for the assistants of freshman senators. In 1961, President John F. Kennedy appointed her director of the U. S. Mint, a position she held until 1969. She has since served on the boards of several corporations.

"If I were to have to choose one individual who, in my political experience in Washington, was the most powerful, I'd chose Eva Adams," Biltz noted in his oral history. "I'd chose her above Senator McCarran because she had that smooth way of getting the job done, and ruffling the fewest number of feathers."

Neither Adams nor Sister Margaret have ever fully gotten over the emotional trauma of going through the postwar immigration policy fight at the side of the man both most admire. They still talk bitterly of the public scorn, and even incidents and threats of violence, that they endured during McCarran's battle over immigration law and for many years after his death. Their voices still lower apprehensively to a near whisper when they talk about the people they still believe to have hatched the plot to discredit the senator, the communists.

Professor Edwards, although often critical of McCarran, believes that in the context of the immigration controversy the senator simply became trapped in a clash of his provincialism with the worldliness of the America's East Coast. McCarran wasn't corrupt or insincere, Edwards says, just very rural in his approach to world affairs. And there was a vindictive, headstrong side to McCarran, he adds, that combined with a similar component in Adams's personality to form a force that can often be "lethal" in politics.

"He didn't understand world realities," Edwards says. "He was a highly skilled and intelligent man who did perfectly well in the United States Senate until this sort of warped view of the world took over in his old

age. I think of him as a victim of his provincial school-
ing and background which served him ill as he went
east. He had as much skill, and ability, and even intel-
ligence as any other senator, but he was a prisoner of a
very provincial background."

Even Greenspun, the columnist who first turned the
big guns of American journalism on McCarran and was
considered the senator's most vitriolic critic, wrote re-
spectfully of the senator in a column marking the senator's death:

> McCarran died as he lived—fighting. He could fight
> in fierce anger, courageously, with the power of a lion or
> he could do battle shrewdly, vindictively, with the cun-
> ning of a fox. And it mattered not whether the cause be
> just or popular. If he had taken a stand to defend it, he
> fought. And who today can say what his motives were,
> because though we may examine a man while he lives,
> it is beyond our power to judge him after death.
>
> There are men who pass through this life barely
> producing a ripple, neither strongly liked nor disliked,
> while others can barely stay afloat in the mountainous
> waves created by the passionate loves and violent
> hatreds which mark their stormy existence.
>
> McCarran was a man of action.

Unlike most contemporary senators, McCarran never
amassed significant personal wealth before or during
his tenure in public office, other than the ranch that his
parents had left to him. Unlike most prominent American political families, his children, grandchildren and
great-grandchildren have not followed the senator into
public office. Having been deeply frightened by the
senator's traumatic encounter with the world outside of
Nevada, it appears, the McCarrans have decided never
to walk that way again.

The Legacy Lives On

The legacy of the encounter of McCarran, McCarthy and Adams with the ever-controversial subject of immigration to America lives on, although the act has been amended several times since its passage. Even in contemporary America, the confused goals of the McCarran-Walter Act cause personal grief to many. In 1989 *New York Times* columnist Anthony Lewis illustrated this by recounting the problems the act had caused for Emil and Judy Suciu.

Mr. Suciu had left Romania for America 20 years before. After arriving in the United States he studied at MIT, then went on to earn master's and doctoral degrees from Boston University. In 1972 he requested permission from the Immigration and Naturalization Service to remain in America.

Under the McCarran-Walter Act, however, he was ineligible for such permission because, in order to become a student, he had had to join the communist party in Romania. The INS denied his request for permanent residence status, but allowed him to stay in America temporarily.

In 1977, Mr. Suciu married his wife, Judy, who was an American citizen and, based on her citizenship, again requested permission to stay in the United States. Once again the INS refused his request.

In 1979, a deportation hearing was held for Mr. Suciu. Four years passed without a decision, and then the judge ordered another hearing, subsequently ordering a background investigation of Mr. Suciu's past in Romania. The report found nothing derogatory.

In 1983, the judge decided that Mr. Suciu's communist party membership in Romania had been involuntary, but then turned down Mr. Suciu's request for permanent resident because the judge said he had been shown classified material that indicated Suciu might be a threat to national security. The judge refused to specify the charges or their sources, citing a clause in McCarran-Walter. Suciu was ordered deported to Romania but he and his wife instead asked Canada to accept them as political refugees and it did.

"All Americans lose when our country acts, out of fear, like the tyrannies we oppose," columnist Lewis noted. "The United States should amend the law to let someone in Suciu's position have a chance at meeting the charge."

Perhaps the most ironic legacy of McCarran's battle against communists, however, are the hordes of economically humiliated people massed along America's southwest border because of the immigration restrictions codified by the McCarran-Walter Act and attempts to amend it. Like the nomadic victims of the Great Depression and the dustbowl days, they certainly are open to the argument that industrial capitalism and the concept of private property are their enemies. Indeed, it is worth pondering how those hungry hordes would react politically if Woody Guthrie, who died in 1967 of the brain-withering Huntington's Disease, were still alive and could stand on a stage along Otey Mesa's anti-immigration trench, belting out "This Land Is Your Land."

The Villain Is Dead

Whether it was real or imagined, the communist threat that energized the passage of the McCarran-Walter Act has nevertheless been officially declared dead.

Perhaps most symbolic of that declaration is the fact that McDonald's could open a restaurant in 1990 just a few blocks from Moscow's Red Square. To mark the occasion, an international team of young people from the United States, Canada and West Germany was recruited to help the new Russian McDonald's employees flip their first burgers beneath Russia's first set of Golden Arches.

Richard O'Mara, foreign editor of *The Baltimore Sun*, described the rise and fall of the communist villain in America well in a cover article for the January 1989 issue of *The Quill*, official journal of the U. S.-based Society of Professional Journalists. The article was entitled "Life Without the Red Menace."

"Americans of my generation have been reared with a 'them or us' attitude toward the Soviet Union," he wrote. "It has colored our views of the world. Some suggest that it has *distorted* our views. The number of politicians who have built careers by exploiting apprehensions Americans have about the Soviet Union, legitimate or otherwise, is beyond counting. Even scholarship about the Soviet Union has been suspect. . . .

"And the mainstream press? Along with many other institutions with pretensions to independence and objectivity, we journalists marched dutifully behind the flag wavers. Since the end of World War II, administrations in Washington, of whatever stripe, have been able to focus our attention virtually anywhere they wished in the world by the simple device of suggesting that the Soviets were active there and that our interests were at stake."

A few months later ultra-folksy columnist and commentator Andy Rooney eulogized the Red Threat that skewed America's immigration policies in an even more succinct way. "Communism has been nice to have around," he noted in an essay for *The New York Times*, "because Americans knew where they stood with communism. They're against it."

CHAPTER 4

The Contemporary Conflict: Family Ties or Skills?

ASKING "WHAT IS AMERICA'S CONTEMPORARY POLICY on immigration?" is like asking "How much does an automobile cost?" The variables are so numerous that there is no one answer. A federal immigration agent pointed out to me once in the late '80s that it was taking about two weeks at that point just for a new agent to be introduced to all the rules—and then the intellectual load was so great that it is impossible for any one agent to remember them all.

Consider, for example, the many immigration restrictions listed in a condensed regulations brochure routinely handed out by the U. S. Immigration and Naturalization Service in 1989.

Being mentally retarded will keep you out, the booklet warns, as will being insane. Those deemed to be "beggars" are prohibited from entering, as are polygamists, homosexuals, drug addicts, drug dealers, alcoholics, stowaways, prostitutes, pimps, draft dodgers, convicted felons, victims of contagious diseases, people who are unable to read and write at least one language, and those arbitrarily deemed "likely to become a public charge."

Communists are forbidden to enter, of course, as are anarchists, Nazis and people believed to be "coming to do extreme violence against our government or people." Also specifically listed in the same collection of forbidden peoples are graduates of foreign medical schools who plan to practice medicine in the United States. (Most members of Congress receive large campaign contributions each year from the American Medical Association, so the practice of medicine is by far the economic turf most explicitly protected by immigration law.)

As soon as you reach the end of this list of taboos, immigration policy takes an even more confusing turn. "Many reasons listed above can be overcome to allow for your admission, either as an immigrant or non-immigrant," says the booklet. "You should contact an immigration office or American Consulate to inquire about waivers and other authorizations."

Among the exceptions are such strange factors as the willingness and ability to invest at least $40,000 in a U. S. business or to do the medical profession's dirty work as a hospital "resident." It is this type of exception, of course, that has caused many naive Americans to wonder aloud why some immigrants own a business shortly after they arrive while many native-born workers can only dream of business ownership, and why few of the emergency room doctors in American hospitals seem to comprehend English very well.

Despite some efforts at simplification, humanization

and rationalization since the passage in 1952 of the McCarran-Walter Act, the laws and regulations governing immigration to America as the country approaches the 21st century amount to little more than a hodgepodge of special exceptions, political compromises, economic barriers, and codifications of fears and prejudices.

The befuddling nature of America's contemporary American immigration law is an immigration lawyer's dream and, consequently, tends to be most lenient to those with the money and sophistication requried to buy their way around the laws. Despite the fact that the country's need for immigrants has always been an economic matter, the policies governing the entrance of those immigrants have never incorporated national economic needs.

Reunifying the Family

If there is any common thread running through America's contemporary immigration laws it is the concept of reunifying families. But it wasn't until about a dozen years after the passage of the McCarran-Walter Act that the family reunification idea was introduced.

No sooner had the McCarran-Walter Act become law than America began tinkering with its immigration policies again. The Refugee Act of 1953, for example, allowed in 214,000 "special" war-affected immigrants, mostly from Europe, but some from Asia as well. To soothe the job-related concerns of the American citizenry, however, the immigrants entering under that act were required to be very close relatives of American citizens or be able to prove that they had a job and housing waiting for them. They also had to be closely screened to ensure that they weren't communist subversives, of course.

In the late '50s, about 30,000 Hungarian "freedom fighters" were allowed to enter, many of them under a so-called "parole" status that allowed Americans to feel that they had taken care of their duty to those Hungarians as fellow anti-communists while not really lifting the country's immigration restrictions. But in 1957 Congress canceled the mortgages on immigration quotas that had been created under the Displaced Persons Act, so America's resistance to immigration was obviously easing a bit as the country's economy grew to full bloom.

After Fidel Castro successfully overthrew Cuban dictator Fulgencio Batista and established himself as the premier of a communist-leaning government in 1959, Cuba's business-owner class began to flee the country in fear of confiscation of its assets and possible persecution by the new anti-capitalist leadership. Again, America made an exception to its immigration laws and about 800,000 Cubans entered. Many of them settled in South Florida, establishing themselves as that region's local shopkeeper class and most effective civic leaders—and thereby planting some of the seeds for anti-Hispanic sentiments of the future.

America's economic boom times of the early '60s mellowed the immigration controversies and rivalries of the '50s somewhat, and the country began to pursue a greater level of humanitarian concern. Then, three younger Democratic politicians who also were raised from Irish-Catholic immigrant roots took Senator McCarran's place as the overriding influence on U. S. immigration law.

President John F. Kennedy brought a new spirit of

egalitarianism to the White House, and that spirit fit well with the newfound wealth of paycheck-class America. His election had been accompanied by the election of a more liberal Congress as well, so in 1962 the Migration and Refugee Assistance Act was passed to allow the Executive Branch greater flexibility in dealing with immigration issues.

Having campaigned heavily on the theme of humanizing immigration policy, President Kennedy then took a bold step further: In July 1963 he proposed a major reform of immigration law that was intended to erase much of the confusion and give the Executive Branch broad powers in adjusting immigration flows to accommodate "the national interest," a term that was intentionally vague. The president envisioned an end to the old system of prejudices and fears that had formed America's immigration policies throughout the 20th century, so he was determined to expunge the old National Origins Act provisions from the federal statutes.

President Kennedy's reform proposal was a "flexible" compromise, Jerry M. Tinker, staff director of the Senate Subcommittee on Immigration and Refugee Affairs, told me in 1989 "It was to level the playing field, in effect, by ending the years of discrimination against Asians, while not setting up new discriminations against those who were the traditional seed countries of immigrants."

President Kennedy's original proposal included minor family reunification provisions, Tinker notes, but didn't emphasize them. But despite President Kennedy's high-minded intentions, political compromise was still required to give his immigration reform bill a chance in Congress, and the eventual emphasis on family reunification was the result of such a compromise.

America of the early '60s was more comfortable than it had ever been since the turn of the century about immigration, but it wasn't comfortable enough just to let the door swing open whenever the president thought it necessary.

The late Abba P. Schwartz, an attorney with an extensive background in international affairs whom President Kennedy asked shortly after his inauguration to take charge of the administration's immigration-reform initiative, told me just weeks before he dropped dead in Brussels in 1989 that family reunification was adopted by the Kennedy Administration as a matter of pragmatism, not idealism. Both John and Robert Kennedy personally asked the dying Representative Walter, McCarran's cohort, for his counsel on the matter.

"Bob Kennedy (then U.S. Attorney General) went to see Walter when he was dying in Georgetown Hospital. I accompanied him," Schwartz told me. "President Kennedy went separately to see him. Walter had one piece of advice: 'You must emphasize family reunification; that's the only way to get the law changed.'"

"That had been (President) Kennedy's view anyway, because in the past he had introduced and gotten some bills through for family reunification. So it was generally accepted that family reunification was the way to finally get rid of the National Origins Act. That's how we got around that, that's how we sold it."

From a political strategy viewpoint, the idea of family reunification is one of those humanly appealing concepts that is difficult for anyone to attack, of course. But the enormity of the political clout of the family reunification concept is often difficult for persons who are of neither Asian nor Hispanic descent to comprehend because it encompasses a subtle-but-essential cultural difference between the earlier immigrant groups and those dominating the flow into America in recent decades.

Unlike the Euro-American cultures wherein heartfelt family ties rarely extend out past siblings and their children, Asian and Hispanic cultures typically nurture and celebrate a family's relationships with people who in the Euro-American cultures would typically be regarded merely as "distant cousins," or great aunts and uncles. Consequently, as the number of Americans of Asian and Hispanic descent has grown in recent decades, the political power behind family reunification has increased geometrically.

"We operate as a family and that is our primary social network," explains Cecelia Munoz, a Bolivian-American who is a policy analyst with the National Council of La Raza, a prominent Hispanic lobbying organization. "For new immigrants, the family is also incredibly important because that is how you adjust to the new country. You're in a new country, a new environment, a new culture, but the family is a piece of your own home."

Even within such tightly knit cultures, however, there is room for immigrant rivalries. Although the National Council of La Raza advocates greatly increased levels of immigration, for example, and is unable to say what the upper limit of liberalization of immigration restrictions should be, it does not want the United States to merely open its borders. To allow such Hispanics as those trapped in Murua to enter at will, the council feels, would drive down wages paid to other recent immigrants to America. "We feel that that approach treats people as a commodity," argues Munoz.

Compromise Becomes Law

Even though President Kennedy heeded Walter's political advice and made family reunification the dominant factor in his immigration reform proposal, the president's initiative was not swept into law. President Kennedy's assassination about four months after he introduced his proposal, combined with strong resistance organized by some less-liberal members of Congress, stalled the evolution of his immigration reform plan into law.

When Lyndon B. Johnson was elected president in 1964, he quickly decided to put his substantial political might behind his predecessor's immigration law proposal. President Johnson resubmitted President Kennedy's proposal on January 13, 1965, amid a flurry of pro-immigration proposals from other politicians. Liberating America's immigration restrictions had become a near fad. Robert Kennedy, by then a senator from New York, and Senator Edward Kennedy, representing Massachusetts, immediately put their immense popular power behind Johnson's immigration bill, of course.

America was feeling wealthy, warm and secure, it had tasted the very intoxicating wine of egalitarianism that President Kennedy had poured so freely. Consequently, it had become more willing than it had been since the start of the Industrial Revolution to share that affluence with the rest of the world.

Despite the pro-immigration euphoria, however, Americans were still quietly worried about new immigrants being a threat to their jobs. Representative Michael A. Feighan, another Irish-American Democrat, had replaced the late Walter as head of the House Subcommittee on Immigration. Feighan's constituency was dominated by the very blue-collar emotions of the heavily unionized Cleveland, Ohio, area, which was populated primarily by people who could trace their roots to 19th-century immigration. So Feighan took a McCarran-like stance, fighting the Kennedy-Johnson forces every step of the way on the relaxation of immigration restrictions and even resorting to accusations of communistic leanings.

Consequently, the final version of the immigration reform bill was still a confused document: It included a mechanism that ostensibly would restrict immigration on the basis of job skills, counterbalanced politically by the system of allowing entrance to relatives of existing Americans to reunify families as Walter had advised the Kennedys would be necessary. Ever the deal-maker, President Johnson was willing to abide by those conflicting concepts if that was what it took to get the then-glamorous bill through Congress.

The new law replaced the old National Origins quotas with an extremely complex and confusing system based primarily on numerous "preference categories" that were divided into various groups by family relationships, through blood and marriage; professionals with skills deemed to be in short supply; a number of other categories of workers; and various types of refugees. Also included were "numerical limitations" (federal staff members were then, and are now, warned against using the stigmatized word "quota") for each country of origin outside the Western Hemisphere, but those numerical limitations, even more confusingly, did not apply to the reunification of immediate family.

The legislation became known as the Immigration and Nationality Act of 1965, and it was signed into law by President Johnson on October 3, 1965, as he stood in front of the Statue of Liberty.

"It corrects a cruel and enduring wrong in the conduct of the American nation . . . ," Johnson said of the bill in a post-signing address delivered in the shadow of America's most venerated symbol of human freedom. "This bill says simply that from this day forth those wishing to emigrate to America shall be admitted on the basis of their skills and their close relationship to those already here. This is a simple test and a fair test."

President Johnson didn't mention that what the bill actually contained was *two* tests that could in no way be coordinated: that of family ties and that of job-skills need in the American workforce. He apparently also had fogotten the words of the Emma Lazarus poem grandly displayed above his head when he added: "Those who can contribute most to this country—to its growth, to its strength, to its spirit—will be the first to be admitted to this land. The fairness of this standard is so self-evident that we may well wonder that it has not always been applied. Yet the fact is that for over four decades the immigration policy of the United States has been distorted by the harsh injustice of the National Origins Quota System. . . . We can now believe that it will never again shadow the gate to the American nation with the twin barriers of prejudice and privilege. . . .

"And today we can all believe that the lamp of this grand old lady is brighter today—and the golden door that she guards gleams more brilliantly in the light of increased liberty for the peoples of all the countries of the globe."

Noticeably missing from the new law and from President Johnson's speech were the concepts of allowing entry to the world's "wretched refuse," its "huddled masses" and the "homeless, tempest-tossed."

While waving the banner of Kennedy-era humanitarianism, America had once again codified its favoritism toward the ethnic origins of its existing residents and its fear of an immigrant assault on its paychecks. It had not expunged the confusion caused by decades of immigration-law tinkering and the subsequent codification of that confusion by the McCarran-Walter Act, but had—for the most part—merely *added* to that confusion.

Since then, a huge industry of lobbyists, analysts, researchers, lawyers and political consultants who spend their days arguing over the various preference categories has grown up around the immigration complexities instituted by the huge compromise championed by Presidents Kennedy and Johnson. It's an industry that does much to enrich the paychecks of those within it, but little for anyone else.

In 1965, America pictured itself as having allowed its golden door of economic opportunity to swing wide once again, but in fact what it was presenting to the world was just another facade of openness, this one gilded with the romantic notion of putting families back together again in America. It was still refusing to acknowledge the fact that immigration had, throughout America's history, been primarily a matter of importing needed labor. Once again the flow of American attitudes toward immigrants had been diverted in the direction of gut emotion, not economic logic.

Overlooked Mathematics

Over and above the confusion and conflict caused in using family ties and job skills simultaneously as criteria for admission to America, the legislation enacted in 1965 contained another big surprise: In their rush to pass something that America of the mid '60s perceived as a return to its immigrant and humanitarian roots, the politicians had forgotten to do their math homework.

The demand for increased immigration among some American ethnic groups, especially those with roots in Asian countries from which immigration had been all but forbidden for decades, was much higher than the formulators of the law had anticipated. For people in many countries, utilizing the new immigration law for all its worth became an overriding family pursuit.

Many native-born Americans of European lineage perceive recent immigrant groups to have arrived in large family units that include complex family trees that extend into several levels of cousins, aunts and uncles. But that perception is, in fact, usually just a mis-observation and/or misunderstanding of the domino effect caused by the potent combination of the concept of family reunification and the determination of many peoples to move to America.

Put most simply, the system usually operates in this way: Foreign-born person A, who may have entered America through some earlier legal mechanism or one of the many one-time exceptions to immigration law, becomes an American citizen independently or, if in America merely on a tourist visa, meets and marries an American citizen (who may or may not be of the same ethnic background, but because of human nature often is) and subsequently becomes an American citizen.

Person A then petitions to have his or her mother and/or father allowed into America as a permanent resident alien. The parent or parents can then choose to work toward citizenship if they wish, but in any case they can then petition to have their children allowed into America by virtue of the fact that they are immediate family of persons legally and permanently residing in America. Those children, the siblings of Person A, are then allowed in, as are their children and spouses, and so forth. Soon, Person A's life in America includes a huge extended family, even though they arrived one-by-one.

What the politicians didn't calculate when they instituted this mechanism was the degree to which it would change both the rate of immigration to America, as well as the rate of change in its ethnic mix. Under the old quotas, based on the ethnic mix at the end of the 19th century, the option of legal immigration often was legally available to people who didn't want to move to America, and unavailable to those who did. But under the 1965 law, the supply of and demand for immigration slots began to intersect.

In the decade following institution of the family reunification provisions, total immigration to America rose nearly 60 percent, and the greatest increases were in the numbers coming from Asia, which sent America 663 percent more people than it had in the previous decade. During that same period net immigration from Europe declined more than 38 percent.

In reaction to the rise in immigration, America began to get upset again, particularly in the South and Southwest, where deteriorating conditions in other parts of the Western Hemisphere were driving out more and more people of Spanish-speaking heritage (who are commonly lumped into the category of "Hispanics" but are really representative of a number of quite varied cultures).

The face in America's mirror was metamorphosing more rapidly than Americans could accept, becoming less and less like the European standard that had for so long constituted the American self-image. Communism didn't seem to be such a threat any more, but all those people with darker or yellowish skin, black hair, a propensity for living in large family groups and un-American tastes in clothing and foods did.

Consequently, in 1976 Congress amended the Immigration and Nationality Act 1965 to impose numerical limitations on the countries of the Western Hemisphere, through which much of this new wave of immigration was coming. But that action, in keeping with the American tradition of clashing immigrant values, collided with the remaining humanitarian instincts and the growing Hispanic and Asian interest-group demands that required America to allow in refugees from political oppression within the Western Hemisphere.

So the amendments continued, and American immigration policy further extended its decades-long excursion into the land of baffling confusion and complexity. Congress reacted to public sentiment again in 1980 by expanding the "political refugee" category, thereby inciting a new era of unresolvable conflict among American ethnic groups over what constitutes an economic refugee versus a political refugee.

Just as it has never been able to formulate a cohesive policy on immigration, America has never really been able to enforce what immigration laws are in effect at the moment. So, with economic and political turmoil spreading in Central and South America in the early '80s, the flow of persons over, under and around America's border barriers continued to grow, and the generous emotions of the Kennedy era began to wane ever more quickly.

By 1986, the fear of such impoverish, "tempest-tossed" immigrants taking American jobs had grown so great, and interacted with racism to such a great extent, that Congress decided for the first time in history to use employers as a key mechanism for the enforcement of immigration restrictions. The law enacted that year made it the responsibility of employers to ensure that the people working for them were in the United States legally.

There is an axiom, "When all you have is a hammer, every challenge looks like a nail"; likewise, job-conscious America decided that jobs were the key to restricting the flow of hungry immigrants.

As a concession to Hispanic lobbying groups, however, the law contained an amnesty provision for people who could prove they had been in America continuously since before Jan. 1, 1982, and thereby allow an estimated 3.1 million people living in America in violation of immigration laws an opportunity to become "legals." But it also created a huge industry in which shady immigration lawyers generate false documents through the creation of shell corporations that purport, for a fee, to have employed would-be immigrants in America since 1981. Various other criminal types charge high fees to sneak people into America and equip them with bootlegged documents, often on an immigrate-now-pay-later plan.

"I told them that I didn't have the money to afford the trip, and they said it didn't matter," a young Salvadoran man residing in northern Mexico told *The New York Times* in 1989 while being interviewed for a story on the booming industry of sneaking people into America. "They promised they would get me across, no matter how many times it takes, and find me a job, and that then I will have to pay them back."

In mid 1989, the man who had headed the INS under President Jimmy Carter told the news media that the employer sanctions enacted in 1986 had accomplished little, other than to buy time for the politicians who had to deal with the controversy of immigration as America entered the 1990s.

"The legislation bought time for everyone and made the problem more manageable for a time," said Leonel J. Castillo, who had become president of Houston International University after leaving government. "It seems, however, that time has passed more quickly than expected, and so it is important to see where we stand, because I think we will be dealing with the issue again soon."

Michael C. LeMay, head of the political science department at Frostburg State College in Maryland and one of the world's leading experts on the politics of immigration, says gut racism was the leading motivation for the passage of the 1986 immigration "reform" law. There are many people from Northwestern European countries who overstay their American tourist visas, he notes, but no one calls for raids on companies that employ them.

"Had our immigration flow not changed in the '70s from northwestern European to Asian-Hispanic, there would not have been a big push in the late '70s and early '80s for a reform of immigration, for employer sanctions. It was an emotional response to the change in the previous flow," he says.

LeMay is one of the very few academicians in the world who specialize in studying the politics of immigration. He is the author of the exceptionally well written *From Open Door to Dutch Door* (Praeger, 1987), an analysis of American immigration policies from 1820 to 1986, and a number of other works that compare the immigration policies of the United States and other countries. In the course of his research he has come to the conclusion that the formulation of immigration law is always an extremely pragmatic process, wherein anxious politicians attempt to balance the unwieldy mix of foreign affairs, social concerns, jobilist fears and humanitarian instincts.

"Immigration policy is not simply a function of any one element at any one period of time," LeMay says. "Something may dominate for a time. For example, in 1965 the civil rights tenor of the country said we have to get rid of the racial overtones of the '20s. The domestic civil rights turmoil dominated the approach used in the '65 immigration act, just as in '52 communism and the cold war dominated the approach they were using. In the 1920s the social-cultural fear of this influx of south-central Europeans who were coming in such great waves and who seemed so different and un-assimilable compared to the Northwestern Europeans brought about the National Origins Act.

"Our internal politics always muck up immigration. Each time you make revisions in immigration policy, what the chief sponsors are tyring to do is to find a new balance. The fact that you have to change the law means that the current policy is being perceived—correctly or not—as no longer achieving what it was set up to do.

"If someone says 'Let's tie immigration to labor market needs,' it will always get sidetracked by this modification and that modification."

McCarran's Successors

As America approaches the 21st century, that syndrome continues to prevail. Because foreign policy is dominated by the Senate—and because immigration law has often been used as a foreign-affairs tool in recent decades—immigration law proposals typically originate in the Senate.

In the 1980s Senator Edward Kennedy, chairman of the Subcommittee on Immigration and Refugee Affairs, and Senator Alan K. Simpson, a Republican from Wyoming and the ranking minority member on that committee, became the primary authors of new immigration legislation, thereby splitting the position that Senator McCarran once occupied as the focal point for America's never-ending immigration controversies.

Kennedy's involvement is an extraordinary political juggling act, according to Professor LeMay. The senator from Massachusetts must continue to play the Kennedy family's political theme song of liberal humanitarianism while attempting to appease the jobilist fears of the labor unions and trying to hold on to the Hispanic vote, all at the same time.

"Kennedy is, to a great extent, carrying on his brothers' involvement and tradition, and that's an important variable with the Kennedys. That's why he is personally so involved," LeMay says. "It also allows him to continue the political link to the Hispanics that Bobby made.

"Kennedy is also very tied in with organized labor and he sees the need for revising immigration law in line with what organized labor wants. He's responding as a leader of liberal Democrats in the Senate, and he's got to come up with a compromise that will not make labor feel overly threatened. But he's also trying to keep the Hispanics happy," LeMay explains.

Simpson, on the other hand, is very much a McCarran-style conservative from the West, a lightning rod for the emotional electricity generated by America's gut resistance to immigrants who don't look, act or speak like those with roots in Europe. He has championed such concepts as requiring that the ability to speak, write and read English be mandatory for anyone wishing to immigrate to America.

"Simpson is involved because he had been chairman of the task force on immigration in 1981," LeMay explains. "He is from an area that is politically conservative and not on the coasts, so you wouldn't think that he would become one of the leading forces in immigration policy-making. It makes sense only that he accidentally inherited this interest.

"He is coming at it from the conservative position. He was the one who wanted the employer sanctions: He saw that we were losing control of our borders, and his reaction was 'What kind of country are we if we can't control our borders?' He is a very practical politician, he has seen the need to change the law, and he's motivated by 'What can we get passed?'

"In Kennedy's case, it's 'What can I sell to labor?' In Simpson's case, it's 'How conservative can we be but still get it through Congress?'"

Immigration guru Tinker, who is widely recognized as the brains behind Senator Kennedy's contemporary immigration-law initiatives, reluctantly confirms LeMay's assessment.

"There's no consensus in this society of what our population growth ought to be," Tinker told me just a few days after the Senate passed and sent to the House yet another immigration law proposal in July 1989. "Let's assume that we want to remain just relatively stable. By the year 2010 you would have a rapidly declining and aging population if you did not have immigration at approximately 500,000 per year levels. At this figure we will not have a rapidly declining population. We'll have an aging population, but the gap will not be so great."

That formula, combined with projections of skills shortage within the American labor market of the '90s and beyond, forms the basis for contemporary American immigration policy. Tinker and his colleagues are striking a compromise between what the American economy needs to stem the process of the work force aging and shrinking, and what the American public can accept emotionally.

Family reunification continues as the dominant theme, while the concept of allowing people to immigrate on the basis of job skills plays a relatively insignificant role numerically—but an increasingly significant role philosophically and symbolically. Despite the passing of more than two decades, the two irreconcilable immigration criteria that President Johnson and the Senators Kennedy blended into the McCarran-Walter Act in 1965 continue in force.

"As we all know, the issues surrounding legal immigration stir deep emotions and strong political passions," Senator Edward Kennedy said in the opening senatorial debate over his new Immigration Act of 1989. "They touch the heart of what America is, how we all became Americans, and who the future Americans will be. . . .

"In short, the pending bill not only carries forward and increases the present emphasis on family reunification, it also opens new opportunities for new immigrants with needed skills."

In reality, those persons who would be allowed to enter America because of their perceived correlation to the work force under that act would, at most, represent 20 percent of total legal immigration. And the limit on total legal immigration that the new bill would set really wasn't formulated on the basis of forecasts of workforce needs.

Indeed, Tinker admits no American immigration legislation—including that which he has helped to develop during more than 20 years as Edward Kennedy's
immigration-law surrogate—has ever scientifically regulated the overall level of legal immigration. The various laws have merely codified de facto immigration
levels: to avoid even greater political conflict, the limits
set have typically been roughly equivalent to the
number coming in legally at the time of the latest bill's
passage.

Legislative rationales for those de facto levels are
then developed retroactively, as evidenced by Tinker's
lawyer-like advocacy of merely *narrowing* the very un-
desirable population-age "gap" rather than *eliminating*
it, which would be the obviously desirable goal.

Tinker argues that Senators Kennedy and Simpson
have, over time, developed sincere interests in immigration matters. But he also points out that the political
community has assigned them the leading roles in the
never-ending immigration conflict because they are
somewhat immune to its political dangers—each in his
own way.

"Anyone in Congress has to be aware of the emotion
and the swirling politics that hamper objective action
in this field," he told me, "but they (Kennedy and
Simpson) are, being from differing political spectrums,
in a unique position to deal with this: Simpson, not
having immigrants not crawling all over him, having a
little freedom to maneuver; Kennedy, because of his
stature, his seniority, his long association with the issue, also being able to withstand some of these pressures of the moment and bring to it a historical perspective, a more balanced view.

"For differing reasons, they're immune to a degree to
many of the political pressures, and are able to bring a

little bit of balance and perspective to it. Both Simpson and Kennedy have that little bit of insulation," he said.

Tinker predicts that as America proceeds toward the 21st century, immigration law will gradually move in the direction of linkages between immigrant skills and work force needs. In the meantime, he and others involved in the setting of immigration policy still spend much of their energy merely buying time and trying to whack the controversy onto someone else's court.

The Immigration Act of 1989, for example, contained a clause requiring the president to reassess immigration policy in 1992, thereby bouncing the controversy toward George Bush at reelection time. From time to time in the late '80s, the U. S. government also was conducting immigration lotteries that would temporarily alleviate political pressure for increased immigration from non-Hispanic, non-Asian countries by allowing 10,000 people at a time to enter merely by the luck of the draw.

"They (Congress) didn't want to deal with the general reforms that were in the Kennedy-Simpson bill, so they temporized by just saying, alright, we'll give a lottery and for those who really want to come here, it at least gives them an escape valve for a period of time while we figure out what we want to do on a more permanent basis," Tinker explained.

The never-ending pressure to allow wealthy and politically connected persons from other countries to buy their way into America was being blunted politically through what Tinker calls a "special earmarking" linked to jobilism. That provision in the latest legislative initiative would allow about 7,000 persons who could invest at least $1 million each in an American-based business—one that would ostensibly employ at least 10 Americans—to enter each year.

In the 1950s the political motivation behind immigration restrictions was the national fear of communism. In the '60s it was the romance of family reunification. But by the start of the 1990s, it had withered to
mere political jousting and the buying of time—to
"temporizing," as Tinker puts it. "We're creeping toward a regular review," he told me in summarizing his
immigration-law accomplishments. To a person using
the breast stroke to keep afloat in the Rio Grande or
Niagara Rivers, of course, every minute of time Tinker
and his colleagues buy is a virtual eternity.

One particularly peculiar aspect of Tinker's perspective on immigration is that he and his policy-formulat-
ing colleagues have felt virtually no pressure in any
direction from American blacks. Many non-black persons opposed to high levels of immigration use the
economic plight of America's urban blacks as a key
argument for immigration restriction; allowing in low-
skilled workers such as those assembled on along the
southwest border, they argue, will create greater competition for low-skilled blacks.

Yet when I asked Tinker in 1989 what opinion America's black community communicates to him and his
staff on matters of immigration reform, he said he
couldn't recall any. "I don't think there's been a serious
articulation of that," he explained.

Government by Obfuscation

Professor LeMay sees the shift toward work force
needs that has been engineered into the contemporary
debate over immigration as merely another politically
expedient device. To a great extent, the concept is politically appealing because it is too complex for the
average paycheck-class voter to correctly comprehend;

all the complex debates, rules and regulations obfuscate the realities.

Nurses, for example, are not very highly paid and do not need to have doctorates, but their jobs can be described explicitly in writing by the American immigration bureaucracy—and foreign-born nurses can, therefore, easily be allowed to immigrate to America under systems that match skills with work force needs. An immigrant nurse could easily fill a job that would otherwise be held by a nurse who was born in America, but the typical American worker doesn't envision the immigration-by-skill concept to include such interactions. To paycheck-class Americans, the new direction of immigration law has gut appeal: It appears to limit immigration only to white-collar types with substantial formal educational credentials. "The person in the street thinks that that type of immigrant isn't going to be competing for their job," LeMay points out.

Steering—or appearing to steer—immigration in favor of the well-trained and well-educated, is likely to be remembered in history the pinnacle of American immigration policy silliness. It is the logical equivalent of founding a country club that accepts for membership only those people who are economically and socially superior to the founders. It ignores the fact that jobs are not a static commodity, that they appear and disappear with increasing rapidity as the rate of technological advancement increases. And it arrogantly overlooks the fact that, although it may be hard to imagine, there may very well come a time when America will not be able to get all the immigrants it needs.

The concept of letting in only the world's best and brightest is, however, one that is—like all of the immigration policies that have preceded it—politically convenient. It is easy for the majority of Americans—many of whom never completed high school, and most of whom do not hold graduate degrees and who do not compete for positions on college faculties, corporate research-and-development teams or government-funded think-tank staffs—to hold the door open to the world's economic elite. Voting for the kind of immigration policy shift that the typical American believes will do that will certainly keep a politican in the good graces of the working-class constituency.

Holding the door open to everyone—even the world's most impoverished and least educated—would, on the other hand, seem to threaten the security of the most cherished possessions of the majority of Americans, their jobs.

CHAPTER 5

Immigrants vs. the American Paycheck

IN 1989, THE AMERICAN SOCIETY for personnel administration issued a strong warning concerning the
U.S. economy of the 1990s and beyond.

A survey of more than 700 human resource management executives by the society had found that nearly
half expect huge labor shortages to develop in the
United States at some point before the end of the 20th
century—shortages of people to perform jobs ranging
from office work, to unskilled industrial assembly, to
skilled crafts.

One respondent predicted that a lack of "hamburger
wrappers in their teens will soon be followed by a
shortage of skilled technicians, professionals and managers."

At about the same time a garment manufacturer in
New England told *The Wall Street Journal* that he was
turning away contracts because it couldn't find enough
workers at its going pay rate of $7.50 per hour, plus
benefits. "I could put 40 people to work today, and

when I filled up my empty machines, I'd buy 30 more machines and hire 50 more workers," he said.

One by one, reports of current and developing labor shortages crop up in America as its population continues to age and the country continues its fight to keep out millions of immigrants who wish to enter and go to work.

Obviously, there's more than enough work in America to go around and then some. So it is logical to ask why Americans continue to resist, resent and, in many cases, plain-out detest the arrival of new immigrants on the basis of fear for the security of their jobs—why the "jobilism" that Professor McKenzie describes has become the national religion, and why such words as "Mexicans," "Koreans," "Cubans" and "Filipinos" are so frequently preceded in America by the word "goddamn."

To a great extent the answer can be found by looking at the relationship between Americans and their jobs *qualitatively* rather than *quantitively,* as is usually the case in the U.S. mass media. In America a paycheck is much more than a statistic, and competition for a paycheck—regardless of whether that competition is real or perceived—is an extremely emotional matter.

You Are Where You Work

It is of utmost importance to observe that in America a job has emotional significance far greater than it would in other technologically developed countries. More than in any other culture on earth, Americans hang the bulk of their self-image on their jobs. In Europe, for example, you can win the respect of your friends and neighbors by being extremely well versed

in, say, world history, or by being known as having
traveled widely—even if you're merely an odd-job day
laborer. In most Asian and Hispanic cultures one's family is a key identification factor. But in America you *are*
where you work, and no amount of knowledge, integ-
rity, sophistication or self-fulfillment can supplant the
need for an identifying and categorizing employment
relationship.

I made this point the theme of the first chapter of *The
Paycheck Disruption,* and since publication of that
book in 1988 I've been approached by many people
who have found much to discuss and ponder in that
contention. But the thought really isn't new, and certainly didn't originate with me.

In fact, no sooner had the Industrial Revolution begun to develop in earnest in the 19th century than some
Americans began to see their wage-working employment situation as an end in itself, with little regard for
the value of the work they accomplished or the satisfac-
tion they gained from it. Back in 1854 Henry David
Thoreau observed: "Most men would feel insulted if it
were proposed to employ them in throwing stones over
a wall, and then in throwing them back, merely that
they might earn wages. But many are no more worthily
employed now."

President Kennedy explored the same syndrome
more politely in *A Nation of Immigrants* (Harper &
Row, 1964), the book he was writing at the time of his
assassination. "In the community he had left, the immigrant usually had a fixed place," Kennedy wrote.
"He would carry on his father's craft or trade; he would
farm his father's land, or that small portion of it that
was left to him after it was divided by his brothers.
Only with the most exceptional talent and enterprise

could he break out of the mold in which life had cast him. There was no such mold for him in the New World."

Without Old World social and economic systems by which to classify themselves, Americans soon learned to correlate their personal status to the size and prestige of their wages. Their paycheck was the only validation of their right and ability to live in America, and they became acutely aware of that.

However, when wage-working first began taking over the American economy in the 19th century, creating New World identities for the earliest waves of mass immigration, it was extremely controversial. Agriculture, fishing, trading and independent craftsmanship had supported most economies throughout history to that point, so political and church leaders of that time repeatedly cautioned their constituencies against the dangers of becoming a "wage slave."

Working for wages—receiving but a portion of the money produced by your work, while the remainder of the money goes to the owner of the machines, land and other capital—was a radical and frightening concept that had arrived full force with the era of industrial capitalism. The prospect of a life of wage-working was so unnerving to Americans of those days that even President Abraham Lincoln was moved to reassure his constituents repeatedly that wage slavery would not be their fate.

By the end of the 19th century, however, a severe depression had beaten down the newly centralized American economy. Such dramatic economic mood swings couldn't occur in the uncentralized economies that existed prior to the advent of wage-working; droughts, natural disasters and pestilence were the major fears back then, and most economies were small enough and isolated enough that when problems arose they remained relatively contained.

So the experience of a national economic disaster was particularly traumatic to the American psyche. Like ancient peoples who panicked during solar eclipses because they thought the world was coming to an end, American wage-workers caught in major economic depressions often could not imagine another bright day. Their panic scared away the arguments against wage-working. Americans had lost their connections to the pre-factory world, and they had no other source of support to which to turn except the emerging world of industry. They were glad when the depression abated and wages began to flow again.

In 1920, the number of people employed in manufacturing exceeded the number working in agriculture for the first time in America, and jobilism soon became the national creed. The Old World village values of education, personal achievement and self-fulfillment had been numbed in this new land of railroads, highways, factories and transient people.

Even Henry Ford, patriarch of the industrial assembly line, lamented the change in human character that was occurring. When not excoriating the Jews for his problems, he often blamed the wage-workers on whom he counted to produce his cars, but to whom he usually condescended. "The average worker, I am sorry to say, wants a job in which he does not have to put forth much physical exertion," Ford said in 1922. "Above all, he wants a job in which he does not have to think."

A Kick in the Teeth

About nine years after Ford made that comment, the Great Depression of the 1930s kicked the American wage-worker in the teeth. Millions of families suffered drastically from that economic dip, and even their still-employed neighbors who watched the jobless grow hungry and homeless resolved that what they wanted most from life was, simply, a job.

The practice of the American government and news media of gauging the country's economic health by merely counting the percentage of people employed and unemployed has further reinforced this attitude, of course. So a half century after the end of the Great Depression, people who earn their living by means other than wage-working in America still experience this unique cultural requirement of an employer-employee relationship frequently—sometimes to the point of frustration.

Failure to submit to the control of an employer—to become what some human resource management experts describe as economically "infantilized"—subjects one to great skepticism in America.

As an independent writer who no longer can cite current employment by a corporate-owned periodical, I'm regularly quizzed by all sorts of people on what I *really* do. If I were an employee of any of the many newspapers or magazines where my work has appeared, that question would never come up, of course. But because my economic life is categorized by the International Revenue Service as a "sole proprietorship," I am treated suspiciously by America's wage-working culture. I also routinely hear of similar experiences from other independent artists, particularly those from other countries who are not accustomed to America's emphasis on wage-working.

For example, in 1989 I attended a concert by Obo Addy, an internationally renowned drummer from

Ghana, on the campus of Oberlin College in Ohio. Because his ability to speak in English is limited—and his culture, like many others around the world, values candor as much as America scorns it—Addy's patter to the audience between musical pieces usually seems blunt and lacks the diplomacy practiced by many American performers. The net result, however, is that he has a way of getting his point across succinctly. On the night that I attended his concert he used this anecdote to vent his frustration with America's paycheck-based culture:

> Often, in America, people come up to me backstage and tell me that they like my music. But then they ask me what I do. I tell them I play the drums. They say, "Yes, but what do you *do?*" And I tell them, "I play the drums, that's what I do." They can't believe that I can make a living playing the drums.

During America's post-World War II boom times this reliance on industrial wage-working presented no problem; indeed, there was little reason to ponder it. A rising tide does, after all, lift all ships, and from the end of the war until the early '70s, America rode the incoming tide magnificently. America's industrial base was the only large one that had not been decimated in the war. What's more, its common currency and language shared by all the states, combined with its relatively low level of economic regulation, had allowed America to become the world's largest mass market. Consequently, the American dollar ruled the world economy, and the average American wage-worker's standard of living improved consistently for about two and one-half decades.

With the wages from a day's work, an American could buy something that required a month's labor to produce in a less fortunate place such as Taiwan. Persons who began life in America as lower working-class immigrants, or the offspring of such immigrants, usually found that the tide pushed them up into the middle class. When economic traumas occurred, such as the oil-supply interruption of the early '70s, the effects were quickly mitigated by deficit spending by the federal government, rampant inflation and expansions in consumer credit. American politicians were able to keep most Americans happy by supporting the rise in the tide. Growth and inflation covered up most political mistakes and abuses.

However, when such tides move back out, as America's began to in the 1970s, things don't always remain so agreeable.

John Higham, a professor of history at Johns Hopkins University, explored the relationship between the comfort level of the indigenous population and openness to immigrants in the preface to the second edition of his historic book on the American nativist movement, *Strangers in the Land* (Atheneum, 1975). "Did social mobility within America actually diminish at the end of the 19th century, and was the society therefore becoming less capable of adjustment to international mobility?" he asked.

Paraphrase Professor Higham's question so that it applies to the end of the 20th century; contrast it to recent research on personal economics in America, and you see that in contemporary context the answer appears to be "yes." Socioeconomic mobility is diminishing in America and the concept of international mobility *is*, therefore, becoming more difficult for many Americans to accept.

The Age of Decline

Yes, the American wage-working middle-class is on the downward track economically—and that very much includes those wage-workers wearing white collars. So many observers talked and wrote about this trend macroeconomically in 1988 that *The New York Times* dubbed them (with more than a hint of skepticism) the "School of Decline."

The American advertising community cannot afford to acknowledge this decline, however, because the large consumer products companies that pay the advertising industry's fees can't afford to acknowledge it. Advertising is the mirror in which wage-working Americans see themselves, so many Americans ironically still see themselves as increasingly affluent. In the pages of America's magazines and newspapers and on its television screens, the human models, the new cars parked on dampened driveways, the suburban homes, the elegant wristwatches, and even the plastic bags used to organize the trash continue to glow in the early morning light that creates the most popular colors on an advertising photographer's pallet.

Most paycheck-class Americans haven't yet noticed that the home mortgages and car loans must keep stretching out over longer and longer periods of time in order to maintain the lifestyles of the '60s and early '70s. They haven't noticed that since the mid '70s a simple economic principle has prevailed: The average cost of living in America quickly expands to consume the average paycheck and only ever-lengthening credit terms allow the typical wage-worker to stay ahead of the syndrome.

For example, home mortgages, which had an average duration of less than five years prior to World War II, stretched out to 30 years by the start of the '80s. In the late '80s they began stretching to 40 years in some housing markets.

Most Americans also fail to notice that affluent living is most prevalent among those people who experienced their prime working years during America's economic heyday, and least prevalent among those just now making their way into the paycheck ranks. People who took an early-retirement buyout from a large corporation in the restructurings of the late '70s and early '80s, for example, often became instantly wealthy; those who are losing their corporate jobs now often get little more than a formal warning not to take any company-owned office supplies with them when they leave for the last time. Americans who bought their homes in the '50s or '60s often can make several hundred thousand dollars in profit now by selling, but their newly married children can't afford a basic bungalow.

Doubting the ability of the American paycheck to maintain its world-class status is, at the very least, considered poor form in the United States. Indeed, academicians who speak in such a way run the risk of being labeled "radical" economists. Some researchers and analysts have, however, begun to work up the courage to publicly link the macroeconomic change in America's global economic status with the microeconomic effects that change is having on individual Americans.

For example, Dick Esterlin, professor of economic demography at the University of Southern California and author of *Birth and Fortune: The Impact of Numbers on Personal Welfare,* pointed out in a 1989 interview with the *Los Angeles Times* that the diminishing economic prospects for America's post-war baby boomers has dissuaded many of them from having chil-

dren, thereby exacerbating the developing labor shortage.

"The deteriorating labor market conditions of baby
boomers have forced them to abandon traditional
norms in a desperate effort to maintain their economic
status," he said.

Robert Reich, a professor of government at Harvard
University, added this perspective in an interview with
the Newhouse News Service on the fate of America in
the 21st century: "Americans will have to sacrifice one
way or another. The task of leadership . . . is to help the
public face its most pressing problems and collaborate
to solve them. Ostrich leadership, by which the leader
tells everyone not to worry and be happy, ends with a
public less capable of taking on the real problems."

The Demise of Credentialling

Another heartfelt effect of America's falling tide is
the confusion and frustration that families who did
prosper in the good times are experiencing in their
attempts to ensure a continuation of their relatively
affluent lifestyles for subsequent generations.

The development of America's economy was unique
in that it was the first time that mechanized transportation enabled huge numbers of people to be delivered to,
and disseminated through, a relatively virgin land mass
abundant with natural resources. As one wave of
human labor after another came ashore and brought
those natural resources to life economically, the aggregate wealth of the nation grew quite consistently—the
only disruption of that pattern being short-lived abatements during economic downturns.

As the collective American wealth grew, many
groups developed systems by which they could accrue

a larger-than-average portion of that wealth to themselves. America's economic system gradually became more structured; its supposedly free-market system of distributing limited goods and services among the unlimited wants of its inhabitants gradually gave way to a system wherein various credentials were used to permanently implant some persons on the higher levels the economic scale.

Naturally, those people who already were in America were better able to utilize and manipulate these credentialling systems than were those who were just arriving. Had there been just one wave of mass immigration to America, or had America never dominated the world economy, the American credentialling system might have succeeded merely in replicating the European economy, wherein there are many elite groups that live generation after generation off the labor of permanent laboring classes that have little hope of upward mobility.

Luckily that was not the case. The growth of America's economic prowess and its population mass was so dramatic over such a short period of time in the context of world history that the credentialling structures created in America merely slowed upward mobility, but never stopped it.

One or two generations of an immigrant family might have had to endure poverty and exploitation, but eventually a generation would break out, attain one credential or another, and move up. Indeed, this breaking-out-through-credentials process is just now being enacted in many American black families that have endured several generations of poverty and exploitation.

The primary tool used in America traditionally has been the college degree. With the exception of a number of societal and governmental schemes devised to keep the black immigrants from Africa uneducated and, therefore, enslaved, public-financed education up to the college level has been provided to everyone since the industrialization of America.

But college has always cost money—often, lots of it—and a college degree therefore provided America's more entrenched population groups with a means of differentiating their offspring economically from those of more recent arrivals, whose formal educations typically would end at some point during the publicly financed stage.

In the immediate postwar period of the 1950s the ranks of white-collar workers were expanding so rapidly that there were approximately 2.5 white-collar positions for every collge graduate in America. Hence, the mere credentialling power of a college degree, irrespective of any knowledge gained through the experience of getting it, virtually guaranteed success through participation in the growing affluence of America's burgeoning corporate managerial class.

America's big industrial corporations had developed the power to accrue disproportionate amounts of wealth to themselves, and those persons who could find a home within the management pyramids of those large corporations usually shared in that wealth. For those who hadn't been able to attend college, trade union membership sometimes provided an alternative route into employment by America's burgeoning industrial-era corporations.

Because everything was on the upswing in America, most people didn't notice that such aggregations of wealth always occur at the expense of someone else; that to allow an auto worker in Detroit to make big money, for example, other people such as a restaurant worker in St. Louis had to drive a beat-up used car, or take the bus. Although the lower-paid workers weren't doing as well as their higher-paid counterparts, their situation continued to improve relatively. The media traditionally focused public attention on the high-end of the job market—such last-gasp aberrations as six-month vacations for unionized steelworkers, for example—and the credentialling system remained politically acceptable.

Many blue-collar workers such as auto and steel workers benefitted enormously from America's boom times, but the really big money and long-term benefits such as stock options and funded pensions were being paid out to the managerial bureaucrats. (Many pensions promised to blue-collar workers were unfunded, making the pensions nothing more than empty promises that now are becoming the responsibility of tax-payer-funded insurance programs.) In the play-it-safe-or-die atmosphere of an industrial bureaucracy one does not take chances by hiring a person on ability or potential; formal credentials, therefore, formed the employment-decision insurance most sought by corporate personnel directors. Only those persons who had completed the requisite college course would be allowed into the corporate white-collar pyramids.

In the 1960s, however, America got carried away with its newfound affluence and, not understanding the interplay between credentials and disproportionate affluence, decided to open the doors of its universities to virtually anyone who was academically acceptable. The concept was based on two very attractive assumptions: First, that college educations would make virtually all those holding degrees economically successful and, second, that the government could lend all the money necessary to students who wanted to attend college but couldn't otherwise afford it.

It was a utopian concept, for sure, but one that was extremely expedient to politicians of the time. Like income-tax deductions for child dependents and home mortgage interest, government-subsidized college educations had no economic logic to support them, but were a sure way to win the votes of the large wage-working class that had developed in post-war America.

Degree Glut

The actual result, however, was a glut of college degrees in the job market. The American economy reached its peak of global dominance in 1973, by most accounts, and it wasn't long before the number of managerial-class jobs began shrinking and the numbers of disappointed college graduates began growing.

Some college administrators were quick to recognize this trend. In the early '80s, while working as a newspaper business reporter, I interviewed a number of small-college senior executives on their strategies for survival in the future. The consensus among them was that to survive in the last two decades of the 20th century and beyond, colleges had to do exactly the opposite of what the typical middle-class wage-working parent would expect.

Instead of expanding and attracting as many students as possible, they told me, colleges needed to *reduce* the size of their student bodies by raising tuitions and admissions requirements, while at the same time attracting record numbers of applicants for admissions. This approach would, they theorized, restore the class-distinction value of the degrees granted by their schools, thereby giving their graduates better-than-average chances of landing one of the increasingly rare management positions.

By attracting huge numbers of applicants, the colleges could be particularly selective and reject record numbers of would-be students. News of the rejections would get around, they said, and that would increase their schools' snob appeal. At no point did any of them bring up the subject of whether or not anyone would be learning to do anything while attending their institutions.

On the other hand, upon entering the workforce, children of lower economic strata—most often, the children of the most recently arrived immigrant groups—coming out of large, government-funded state universities and community colleges would be easily spotted and would not compete easily against those getting their degrees from the less-attainable institutions. In the '80s, '90s and beyond, they said, it would require a *prestigious* degree, not just a degree, to ensure economic superiority. Their schools could charge high prices for that prestige, thereby ensuring the continued existence of the small colleges.

The college administrators' strategy has, obviously, been implemented. The headlines in American newspapers of recent years have included innumerable accounts of rapidly rising college tuitions, the high cost of multiple college admissions applications, and even of long-term investment programs that allow parents to prepare for tuition bills that will be exceeded only by their mortgage payments. The articles naively explore these developments as though they are unavoidable Acts of God.

Already, however, history is repeating itself: Just as government-sponsored student loans were the rage in the '60s and '70s, when inflation quickly diminished most long-term personal debts, government-sponsored tuition savings and investment programs for anxious parents proliferated during the relatively low-inflation years of the late '80s. Once again, politicans have found a way to win voter approval by financing college educations, even though the effort is inherently self-defeating in an economy operated by credentialism.

There is one other effect of America's credentialling traditions that is, perhaps, the most profound: As each wave of immigration threatened the economic dominance of the preceding one, the barriers into lucrative professions and occupations were built higher and higher. Occupations that once required only a high school diploma now required a college degree. Professions that once required only a two-year college certificate, such as teaching and nursing, now often require four-year degrees.

Now that these barriers have been under construction for more than 100 years, their extreme height has left most Americans in the precarious position of not being able to restart their lives easily after experiencing an economic trauma. How many can afford to take a work break of several years to go back and get a new college degree or work their way up into a new craft? That which went around has, as the axiom goes, come around.

James Fallows, Washington editor of *The Atlantic Monthly*, describes this situation well in his book *More Like Us* (Houghton Mifflin, 1989), which explores American culture in contrast to that of Japan.

"With the rise of educational requirements and licenses, the [American] formula for success changed," he wrote. "How someone prepared for a job became at least as important as how well he actually did it. . . . To see how harmful it can be to American mobility, think again of the steelworkers. Because they had not stayed in school 10 or 20 years earlier, it was impossible for them to start over in a number of jobs in which they might have been able to succeed."

To drive his point home, Fallows uses the growth of America's wide-open, unstructured computer industry—the most legendary founders of which were college drop-outs—in the 1980s as an example. "Imagine the condition of the American computer industry today if hardware designers and software engineers were licensed, like accountants, and had to pass a qualifying exam drawn up by IBM," he suggested.

Barriers Are Hard to Find

With the comfortable bureaucracies of industrial America evaporating along with the country's global economic dominance, and the power of college-degree credentialling slapping itself to death like a once-full sail luffing into the wind, the upper echelons of the American economy are finding it difficult to resurrect the barriers to entry to various careers and professions that controlled the American economy and distributed wealth disproportionately during the country's industrial boom times.

Consequently, professional licensing has become the last economic foxhole; indeed, when one sees someone driving a very expensive car in America today, it is immediately assumed that the driver is a licensed professional—an accountant, a lawyer, a dentist, a physician, or the like.

But even the option of becoming a physician, which was the most lucrative license-based alternative to corporate careers in the '60s through '80s, has diminished dramatically in its economic potential. Because America can no longer afford the burden of ever-rising medical bills, most young physicians now enter the world of work as employees of some type of healthcare-cost management organization, not independent business people, and at salaries that are not much higher than those paid to many people who have never set foot in a college classroom. In 1988 the *New York Times* reported that the typical newly licensed American physician was starting work at an annual salary of about $35–40,000.

What's more, the popularity of filing malpractice suits against the greedy physicians of the previous generation has grown to the point that a person watching television in America is as likely to see an advertisement for attorneys anxious to help them sue their physician as for a car dealer wishing to sell them a new mode of transportation.

The only economic refuge many affluent families have been finding (or, at least, think they are finding) for their offspring is the American legal cartel. America's legal cartel has, to a great extent, replaced the industrial corporations as the segment of the American economy most able to accrue disproportionate revenues to itself. Consequently, students who might have pursued an education in business administration forty years ago to qualify for a place in the corporate bureaucracy now frequently opt for law school.

Each year thousands of baby boomers who took a troubled wrong career path early on and have failed to find any kind of material success decide to go to law school in a mid-life attempt at economic self-rescue. The practice of law is becoming the white-collar career of last resort in America; he (or she) who would have chosen to be William H. Whyte's corporate "Organization Man" of the 50s is now the Legal Cartel Man (or Woman).

Lawyers have a unique position in the American

economy in that only they have direct access to the democracy's justice system. Banded together into quasi-governmental guilds they call "bar associations," self-policed, protected from interlopers by government-enforced licensing regulations and conducting their business in intentionally arcane language unintelligible to non-attorneys, they have no external competition. Theirs is a cartel that controls a unique and emotional commodity—the power to put you in jail, for instance, or to grant or deny you custody of your children, or to cut themselves in on a substantial percentage of the few dollars of life savings that your mother left to you at her death.

One product of this cartel is the fact that the legal profession includes what is apparently the greatest concentration of criminals in America outside of prison walls. I was introduced to this sad fact while a rookie reporter in the early 1970s. During my first stint as a courthouse reporter I noticed that virtually every time someone was charged with the crime of failure to file a federal income tax return, the defendant was an attorney.

Isn't it odd, I thought in my state of naivete, that attorneys would *forget* to file their income tax returns? Surely, they of all people must be aware of the need to do such things in a timely fashion. Eventually I was moved to ask a courthouse old-timer what was going on.

It was a simple, time-honored scam, he explained: Attorneys know that it is a serious offense to lie on their federal tax returns, but a relatively minor offense to fail to file—particularly since, if caught, they can argue that they merely forgot or were confused and thought they had filed. And, unlike the average American, they know that the agents of Internal Revenue Service don't spend their nights and weekends memorizing your social security number and income statistics—that the chances of the IRS noticing the absence of your return are relatively slim.

Consequently, when they have a particularly profitable year, many attorneys "forget" to file their income tax return and hope that no one at the IRS notices. If someone does notice and accuses them of criminality, the attorneys simply argue that they forgot to file and then pay the money that they would have had to pay anyway. Unlike non-attorneys, they don't need to hire a lawyer who is going to send a big bill whether you're convicted or not. But if, as the odds dictate, no one at the IRS notices, the forgetful lawyer enjoys a tax-free year.

The Sleaze Tour

Because of the nature of my work, I've endured more time in the company of attorneys than anyone should have to in several lifetimes. Consequently, I've been treated to the grand tour of American sleaze. The criminal disposition of many attorneys is such that I've seen them do dishonest things over amounts of money that most other people wouldn't even bend over to pick up if they saw it lying on the sidewalk. For example, I have seen them tear off the "To:" portion of the address label on a package of items sent to them for review and then drop the package back into a mailbox, thereby saving themselves the few pennies of postage necessary to return the package to the party that sent it.

Their greed often has no ethical bounds: While working as a communications consultant in the mid '80s, I watched a group of small-town, politically affiliated attorneys rape the treasury of a small hospital. By the time they were finished pillaging, the hospital was so short of money that it had to lay off a substantial number of support people such as nurses' aides who help to make hospitalization somewhat humane. Witnesses to such acts are helpless, as I was in that situation, because the only people you can report such attorneys to is their private protective organization, the bar association.

Even though I am painfully aware through experience of the criminality that permeates America's legal community, I have never had the time or resources that would be required to quantify the extent of the level of criminal activity among American attorneys—although I must admit that my journalistic urges make we want to. In 1989, however, the New York State tax department accomplished just such a quantification.

Through a survey, the tax people found that nearly 10 percent of the partners in New York law firms—many of them earning about $1 million a year—failed to file a return for at least one of the previous three years. Almost 350 of them hadn't filed a return in any of the previous three years. And although failure to file for three years constitutes a felony in New York, and consequently is supposed to result in removal of an attorney's license to practice law, there was no record of any such action against the tax-dodging attorneys.

The survey found, in contrast, that among the non-attorney employees of those same law firms, only one half of one percent had failed to file their state income tax returns.

The American legal community is as selfish as it is corrupt. In 1989, for example, a panel specially appointed in New York State to study the availability of legal representation to the poor found that, despite the burgeoning number of attorneys, the availability of legal counsel to the lower economic classes was diminishing.

"The poor need legal help to obtain basic human requirements and to an appalling degree cannot get it," said the panel's report. "It is grotesque to have a system in which the law guarantees to the poor that their basic human needs will be met but which provides no realistic means with which to enforce that right."

In reaction to its study, the panel recommended that all attorneys in that state be required to donate a mere 20 hours per year to public service. But, as had been the case when earlier legal reform groups had made such proposals, the lawyers launched a huge campaign opposing the panel's proposal.

Since judges and most elected government officials in America are laywers, the power of the legal cartel to raise money for itself while ignoring the law is virtually unlimited; reform will not come soon, if ever. Enduring the abuses of the legal cartel is, perhaps, the price America will always have to pay for being a country of laws, not men.

The saddest fact, however, is that the corrupt and unethical world of the American attorney is becoming *attractive* to an increasing number of Americans: In 1988, for example, American law schools experienced a rise of 18 percent in the number of applications for admission, compared to the previous year. In 1989 the increase was 22 percent over the previous year.

"Last year it seemed that the increase might be an aberration," Edward Stern, a lawyer who advises undergraduates at Boston University, told a reporter in 1989. "But now it looks like a trend."

"There is now the perception that legal training alone will allow you to make money," added Dean Gerald Wilson of Duke University.

That is, however, merely a perception. The value of a cartel to an individual participant resides, of course, in its ability to minimize internal competition as well as that from outside interests, and that is where the American legal community has failed itself. Unlike organized medicine, the legal cartel has not succeeded in sufficiently limiting the number of its members; amazingly, it has not even tried to do so to an effective extent, as the American medical profession has for decades. I knew the legal community was failing in that goal the day I found a promotional newsletter in my mailbox from the one attorney I trust to some degree right next to a newsletter from my dog's veterinarian.

To a certain extent, the amount of legal activity has expanded to accommodate the number of lawyers available, resulting in what is now described as the "litigation logjam," which often causes even simple cases to take several years to resolve. But the expansion hasn't been quick enough to fill the career-option gap left by the demise of the large industrial structures. Although the aggregate number of dollars flowing to the legal cartel is increasing, the bounty is being diluted by the huge number of people entering the profession.

From 1972 to 1987, legal services was the second fastest growing service-producing industry in the United States, according to the U.S. Department of Commerce. The legal community also set national records during that period for rapidly rising prices and declining productivity: measured in inflation-adjusted dollars, the typical attorney produced in 1987 only half of what he or she would have produced in 1972. Such is not a scenario that will lead to rising affluence in the future, of course. In any industry, lower productivity eventually leads to lower incomes.

Certainly there are attorneys who still make huge incomes and will continue to do so. But, with few exceptions, they accomplish that only by exploiting huge numbers of employee attorneys at the bottom of their practice pyramids. In most cases the prosperous ones, or their fathers or grandfathers, were in the profession long before the parents or grandparents of many contemporary Americans had come ashore.

Consequently, approximately 40,000 American lawyers are abandoning the practice of law each year, and that number has been growing. It's almost equal to the number entering the legal profession, and the defectors are being described by career-market economists and others as "alienated labor."

"There is no doubt that many lawyers, particularly young ones, are alienated labor," wrote *New York Times* legal affairs columnist David Margolick in 1989. "Whatever prompted them to enter the profession— idealism, status, intellectual curiosity, skills training, *the lack of a clear alternative* [emphasis added]—many are appalled at what they've found."

With the economic power of formal educational credentialling in decline, and the two most lucrative licensed professions in economic turmoil, white-collar American wage-workers are having a difficult time putting form and structure to their economic lives and those of their children. Indeed, in the case of those looking toward the practice of law as an economic refuge, they are being forced to decide what level of criminality they are willing to risk and abide in order to maintain their family's lifestyle. But the decline of the prospects for the American paycheck worker is afflicting the blue-collar classes, as well, and at that level the problems can be even more stinging.

Can't Go Home Again

There are tremendous emotional consequences in the decline of the American paycheck for America's less-affluent working classes. For them, it is much more than a matter of having to drive a Buick rather than a Jaguar.

For example, rank-and-file Americans are starting to look longingly toward home again, according to an analysis of public sentiment by *Good Housekeeping* magazine in 1988. The post-war decades took America on an odyssey of social and political adventures that included waves of child bearing, then social idealism, then materialism. But in the 1990s and beyond America will, according to *Good Housekeeping's* research, become a country of "new traditionalists" who value family and home life above all else. After all these adventures, it seems, the baby-boomers want to go home.

That sounds like good news. Certainly, many paycheck-class Americans would welcome some time out from the breakneck pace of work and material acquisition that kept them dashing about in the final stretch of the '80s. But the sad truth is that the 1990s and beyond are destined to be a time of unprecedented frustration in United States because, like it or not, paycheck Americans can't go home again.

The bad economic habits that developed during America's post-war boom times have left America in a position where a warm, fulfilling home life is something most people simply can no longer afford. Contrary to the ubiquitous images of affluence that emanate from the advertising community, the median household income in America in 1988 was just slightly more than $30,000 per year, about seven percent lower today than 10 years before, in inflation-adjusted dollars. The growing number of households headed by a single woman had an average income of just slightly more than $13,000, according to Census Bureau figures.

The presence of a second wage earner in an American household is no longer an optional means of upward mobility, according to the Census figures, but a necessary defense against looming downward mobility. Women are approaching wage parity with men mostly because men's wages have, on average, been declining since 1973. And at least one-third of the American workforce is now classified as "contingent," meaning that they're not covered by health insurance, unemployment insurance or any other type of security-building employment fringe benefit.

Certainly, some wage inflation has been taking place at the lowest end of the wage schedule because of the growing shortage of unskilled and low-skilled labor, but the move from $4 to $7 per hour hardly qualifies one as newly affluent. Indeed, most statistical analyses that seem to show increases in blue-collar incomes are actually reflecting primarily the increased cost of company-paid healthcare coverage. And healthcare coverage is something that many companies are abandoning by creating "contingent" work relationships or requiring their employees to begin paying for some of it.

Meanwhile, the ability to purchase homes is rapidly eroding. In some parts of America, such as the San Francisco Bay area, average home prices had, at this writing, reached a multiple of 10 times average household annual income; about three times annual income has long been considered the upper limit of responsible fiscal behavior. Some major companies have been helping their employees to purchase homes by creating "equity sharing" programs that come frighteningly close to the old "company home" systems utilized by mills and mines in the darkest early days of the Industrial Revolution.

Politicians have responded to this problem by creating a federally insured program that would allow young couples to purchase homes under a system based on what is known euphemistically as "negative amortization," but which really means that the amount the home purchasers owe would grow each year for at least the first 10 years of the mortgage. The ability to eventually pay off the growing debt is based on presumptions of a continuation of the wage and home-price inflations of the '70s and early '80s—both of which had ended prior to the drafting of the bill.

Even those Americans who can still afford to purchase homes are watching the size of their living space shrink. In New Jersey, for example, former single-family suburban homes are being divided into multiple housing units in a last-ditch effort to provide middle-class workers with housing that at least resembles the American Dream of the '50s and '60s.

New automobiles have remained affordable to many families only through long-term financing arrangements that, as the *Wall Street Journal* pointed out in 1988, frequently leave families economically "upside down," that is, owing more than their used car is worth.

In this turbulent economic climate, the basic pleasure of a tranquil family life is disappearing so quickly that some mothers were discovered by the *Los Angeles Times* to be clandestinely leaving their pre-school children unsupervised in public libraries each day in a desperate attempt to keep them safe while Mom puts in her eight hours on the job.

What's more, the Census Bureau reported in 1988

that for the first time in American history more than half the mothers with babies less than one year old are remaining in the job market. In response, some cities began considering government-sponsored infant day care programs as a means of attracting residents from the increasingly harried paycheck class.

The declining fate of the American wage-worker can also be seen in the diminishing quality of work situations. In mid 1989, for example, the National Safety Council reported that the number of permanent physical disabilities resulting from work-related accidents was climbing dramatically, apparently as a result of increasing pressure on workers to perform more quickly and over longer periods of time.

It's obvious, sentimentality aside, that most Americans no longer have the freedom to return to the home-and-family values that their parents enjoyed during the country's industrial boom times. Americans have encumbered themselves well into the 21st century based on the long-term, steady paychecks that are becoming so difficult to find now that America no longer controls the world's economy.

Peter Morrison, director of the Population Research Center at the Rand Corp., a think tank, points out that the changing economic fortunes of the typical American wage worker can be seen most dramatically in the fact that Americans can now be divided into groups of housing "haves" and "have nots": Those who purchased their first home in the '50s and '60s before the huge increases in house prices, and those who bought one after the housing price escalation had developed full force.

The early home buyers make up that affluent group of older Americans that retailers are chasing with increasing enthusiasm. Through mortgage payments and taxes, the children of those people make up the generation that must now pay the bill that their parents, the first and last *affluent* generation of American wage workers, accrued.

Frank Levy, an economist in the School of Public Affairs at the University of Maryland and author of *Dollars and Dreams* (W.W. Norton, 1987), explored the economic generation gap further in a 1989 interview with the *Wall Street Journal*.

"When incomes are growing fast," he said, "inequality has less meaning because the poor are getting richer and the rich are getting richer even faster—but everybody's better off. Because of the general stagnations of earnings in this decade, that's not the case now.

"A relative decline means an absolute decline. The sharpest example is that if you look at workers in their late 20s and early 30s with a high school education, in the early 1970s they were averaging $22–23,000 in today's dollars and today they are making $18,500."

The structures erected within the American workplace served in many ways to diminish the intensity of immigrant rivalries during the 40 years following World War II. During the boom times, various groups were able to stake a claim through credentialling—and through other barriers to participation in various occupations, such as union membership—to the piece of the ever-growing economic pie that they preferred. Even unskilled sweat laborers often were able to move up into the middle class without adding to their skills or abilities.

But that, as we've seen, is no longer the situation. One tragic result is the growth of cynicism among rank-and-file Americans. For example, a nationwide study released in 1989 by Boston University professor Donald Kanter and organizational behavior specialist Philip

Mirvis found that 43 percent of America's working population had come to believe that "lying, putting on a false face and doing whatever it takes to make a buck" are part of basic human nature.

Considering the emotional nature of this ubiquitous decline, it is not surprising that the typical paycheck-class American sees hungry new immigrants as a threat and is pleased by legislative proposals that would seem to keep the hungriest of the world on the other side of America's borders. When it appears that there's not enough food in the pot to feed those already seated at the table, how can one invite still more people to dinner?

CHAPTER 6

The Rational Option: Let Prosperity Follow Where Immigrants Go

WHAT IF YOU AWOKE one day and encountered a magical morning when all the rules of the universe were turned topsy-turvy? A bright sun would be rising in the West, nurturing raindrops would be falling from clear blue skies, cats and robins would be frolicking together in your garden, and the ads in the morning newspaper would indicate that the price of a pure wool suit was one fourth of that of one woven from strands of recycled plastic milk jugs.

And what if you then discoverd that merely by grinding up coffee beans to put into your brewing machine, you were causing great new coffee plantations to spring up; that by merely eating the food on your breakfast plate you were causing farm animals to be born and vast fields of grain to sprout from the ground; and that just by drinking your orange juice, you were turning acres of former swampland into verdant citrus groves?

And then what if you then looked at the front page of your morning newspaper and encountered a huge headline that said: "Immigrants don't consume prosperity, they create it?"

To most Americans, that headline could be true only in a fantasy world; but in truth, the fantasy ended when breakfast was prepared. Standard wisdom notwithstanding, those who study the American economy scientifically know that both consumption and immigration *add* to America's affluence, rather than *subtract* from it. In a consumption-based economy such as America's, ever-rising consumption has always been the seemingly magical force that makes wonderful things rise from the bare earth.

There are mountains of evidence that there will never be too many people seated around the table, as most American adherents to the religion of jobilism believe would be the case if America's borders were opened. All the attempts at legislating immigration restrictions have been unnecessary exercises in political pandering. There is no need to maintain an ever-growing immigration bureaucracy.

With a new dose of mass immigration flowing through the country's veins, the decline of the average American's standard of living could be reversed. America needn't forsake its immigrant heritage to survive; it is not necessary for people of less fortunate lands to suffer and die along America's borders so that Americans can prosper. The discussion of immigration need not be a matter of shameful racist emotions disguised in pompous rhetoric; a politician with enough guts could champion open immigration and survive proudly to take credit for the results.

Despite overwhelming evidence that prosperity follows where immigrants go, one generation after another of Americans has come to believe that each arriving wave of immigrant labor somehow diminishes the material wealth of those already situated within the country.

Politicians have, as we've seen, continually exploited that fallacy by passing one irrational, disjointed, insincere immigration law after another. Equipped with virtually no understanding of economics, the majority of Americans have reacted favorably to the emotion-based immigration restrictions those politicians effected. To do otherwise would seem as foolish as an attempt to reverse the laws of gravity.

The idea that open immigration is the key to a resurgence of America's economy—and, consequently, a resumption of the material improvement of the America lifestyle—seems radical to most Americans. But it's not at all radical to those familiar with the forces that drove America to its world dominance of the 1950s and '60s. Indeed, even the very mainstream *Wall Street Journal*, hardly a voice of economic iconoclasm, promotes open immigration as the keystone of a new era of economic success.

To celebrate Independence Day 1989, for example, the *Journal's* "Review & Outlook" section reprinted Emma Lazarus's' Statue of Liberty poem about immigrants in full, lamented the fact that immigrants were being hounded at work, then commented, in part:

> Three years ago today, we offered an alternative. We wrote, "If Washington still wants to 'do something'

about immigration, we propose a five-word constitutional amendment: There shall be open borders.

We added, "Perhaps this policy is overly ambitious in today's world, but the U.S. became the world's envy by trumpeting precisely this kind of heresy." A policy of liberal borders is no more or less radical than the notion that a democracy founded in a new, wild world could become the envy of all nations. . . .

This nation needs the rejuvenation that recurrent waves of new Americans bring. Latins, Vietnamese and West Indians are the new Irish, Italians and Poles. We must guard against slipping into the self-satisfied view that we are good enough as is, no more need apply or trespass on the American experiment.

Such advocacy occurs rarely, if ever, in America's nonbusiness news media. Indeed, with the exception of the *Wall Street Journal* and a few other relatively sophisticated business periodicals, America's news media have served as loyal disciples of the jobilism that supports most contemporary resistance to immigration. And many people who consider themselves to be business leaders, and can therefore be presumed to be somewhat familiar with the economics of work, exacerbate the fear of immigration by holding jobs as public relations hostages: They routinely threaten to eradicate jobs if the government doesn't provide the subsidies their businesses demand, and the news media routinely echo those threats.

To at least some extent, the level of misunderstanding of economic cause-and-effect has become worse now that television news has become Americans' dominant source of information: Economists have never been good at simple explanations, and when it comes to explaining the advantage of immigration to the U.S. economy, they just can't come up with the essential short, succinct, declarative sentences—the "sound-bytes"—by which television journalism lives.

"Human Capital"

One of the most frustrated of such economists is William B. Johnston, vice-president of special projects at the Hudson Institute and project director for the writing of Workforce 2000, the most highly regarded and frequently quoted study of the future of the American labor force produced in the 1980s. Although Workforce 2000 originally was conceived merely as an academic study funded by the U.S. Department of Labor, more than 50,000 copies of it have been sold to American business owners, managers and others concerned about the future availability of workers. Workforce 2000 reminded corporate America that in the contemporary world of business, people are the most important commodity.

"As the miraculous rebirth of Europe and Japan after World War II has proven," the study pointed out, "the foundation of national wealth is really people—the human capital represented by their knowledge, skills, organizations, and motivations. Just as the primary assets of a modern corporation leave the workplace each night to go home for dinner, so the income-generating assets of a nation are the knowledge and skills of its workers—not its industrial plants or natural resources."

In introducing the Immigration Act of 1989 to the U.S. Senate in 1989, Senator Kennedy cited Johnston's research as the key element in the shift toward coordinating immigration law with workforce needs. The act "recognizes future U.S. labor needs, especially skilled professionals, as documented in the Department of

Labor's study, *Workforce 2000,* by adding additional opportunities for immigrants qualifying in these fields," Kennedy said.

However, despite the fact that Johnston's advice and economic projections have become virtual gospel truth in many of America's corporate boardrooms and on the floor of the Senate, he hasn't been able to drive home his advocacy of increased immigration.

"I have struggled to articulate this in a way that it is as overwhelmingly persuasive to other people as it is to me, having looked at the numbers and tried to think through who wins and who loses," Johnston told me during a 1989 conversation in his office just outside Washington, D.C. "There is a giant gap between what economists think about this subject and what most other people think about this subject. There may not be any simple analogies that can make this clear.

"I've looked at all the evidence that exists, and all the evidence says immigration benefits us."

In an attempt to explain his findings on immigration to interviewers trained at the "School of Jobilism," Johnston has developed one illustration of economic subtleties that makes his point quite well. He calls it his "Tale of Two Cities."

"Look at Detroit and then look at Los Angeles," he suggests. "There are a lot of different things going on in those cities, but one aspect of the bottom line is that there are very few immigrants in Detroit and over-whelming numbers of immigrants in Los Angeles. And yet Los Angeles is a much better place to find a job, and it has a much faster growing economy than that of Detroit.

"Immigration has not swamped Los Angeles. It has made Los Angeles a bigger, more vibrant place than it has ever been before—on its way to becoming the capital of the Pacific. The lack of immigration, on the other hand, hasn't saved Detroit from the problems it has because of the ups and downs of the automobile industry."

The idea that mass immigration, much of it from impoverished countries, has been a major component in the development of America's most glamorous metropolis doesn't sit well, of course, with America's tradition of resenting new immigrants and blaming problems on them. Johnston acknowledges that.

"We have a 200-year history of everybody resenting the new immigrants. Every single wave has been objected to, whether it was the English objecting to the Irish or everybody hating the Poles and the Italians," he says. "And then they [the new immigrants] become valedictorians and business owners and leading citizens and then, looking back after 40 years after those immigrants' kids all speak perfect English and their daddies all own businesses, people realize that it all worked out very, very well."

Americans have created this tradition, Johnston believes, because they have never understood the simple fact that the success of one economic group does not necessitate the failure of another. "The economic evidence is overwhelming that immigration benefits this country. It always has, and it does now," he says. "But people looking at it don't always see that part of the equation. They see people who speak another language and act differently. They see people who compete for what they perceive to be their group's job opportunities—they perceive competition.

"Most people see it as what an economist calls a 'zero-sum game': If the immigrant wins, I lose. But that's not true. The benefit of a Hispanic taking a job in a kitchen, for example, turns out to be that he makes money, buys a car, buys his meals at the McDonald's down the street and all of those things that mean more growth later on," he says.

Even today, Johnston points out, the age-old argument that immigrants drag down wages and, consequently, the lifestyle of existing American workers survives.

"The one area where there is [economic] debate is what happens to manufacturing wages in areas where there are very large numbers of immigrants. People who study this closely say, yes, maybe it does hold manufacturing wages down a little bit," he notes. "But that is a very small impact compared to the overall impact on job creation and the overall welfare of America."

Johnston has found through his research that international borders and the restrictions that usually surround them have less and less meaning in America's increasingly global economy.

"If Mexico was filled with talented managers and engineers, and America was filled with people who only knew how to tighten bolts, the palm trees would be south of the border," he says, alluding to the *maquiladoras* springing up along America's southwest border. "The work has flowed to the competence of the people, and that is true all over the world.

"You can do more with the Mexicans if you bring them up near some American managerial capabilities and nearer to the American market. Consequently, those people are far richer than they would be otherwise. But that doesn't mean that we're far poorer, any more than it did when United Fruit six or seven decades ago went to Honduras and turned the jungle into banana plantations. America wasn't worse off because of that; now it had bananas. The Hondurans finally had jobs that produced wages that bought far more for them. Both sides were gainers.

"There's not a dime's worth of difference between what happened then and what's happening now. Through the use of organization, education and financial capital, we can create far more wealth."

But what if the Mexicans who are piling up in places such as Murua and, consequently, being sentenced to work forever for low wages in the *maquiladoras* were allowed to come into America? Would they be a threat to Americans?

No, says Johnston. The newly arrived workers would, however, be earning their wages—and spending most of that money—in America, and that would be a beneficial development.

"Things wouldn't be very much different, except perhaps that land would be worth a bit more on this side of the border. America would be a little bit richer, because our population would grow a little faster and we could collect more taxes," he points out. The same would be true, of course, if other exploited low-wage workers farther away, such as those in places like Taiwan that assemble much of what Americans buy, were allowed to flow into America.

One of the most commonly raised points in discussions of America's contemporary immigration policies is that many immigrants to America arrive illegally, skirting American law in attempts to find a better life. Whenever that point is raised, it adds an implication of criminality to the concept of an immigrant. It tends to steer the discussion away from economic considerations and toward the effectiveness and appropriateness of police activities directed at the immigrants ominously labeled "illegal aliens."

But Johnston's advocacy attacks even that well-entrenched concept. Immigrants who enter America illegally, he points out, often energize the American economy even more than their colleagues who arrived within the parameters of American immigration law.

"As evidenced by the border closing efforts, America doesn't like illegal immigration," he says. "But from the viewpoint of an economist, illegal immigration is the best kind of immigration in certain respects because those people have to leap a high hurdle: they have to break the law and leave everything behind in order to find work.

"That automatically gets you a self-selected group of people who are very highly motivated. Illegal immigrants have always been the motivated, the most chance-seeking people, and that's what this country's always been about."

Johnston also emphasizes a point that has long been discussed in relation to marketing strategies, lifestyles and government benefit programs such as Medicare but is just beginning to be applied to the discussion of immigration restrictions: Americans are, on average, becoming older, and there are significant implications to that fact.

"This has always been a young country, and it stands great risk of becoming a middle-aged country. It is certainly, in absolute terms, going to be a lot older in the next century. As far as the eye can see, America is getting older, and older people are more set in their ways than young people," he explains.

"You can look at census statistics that show that people in their 40s or 30s change occupations or locations less often than people in their 20s, or you can look at it in terms of industrial dynamics where you have older organizations: AT&T, average age mid-40s, up against MCI, average age mid-20s. This particularly plays out in the airlines and computer companies.

"Immigrants are young in every sense, in the absolute sense as well as in that sense that they have to learn things that are brand new. They are, therefore, much more flexible about the way they approach the world. That's very much to America's benefit."

Overall, Johnston predicts a growing gap between the demand for human labor in America and the supply available, in terms of both quantity and quality. Of course, he and organizations such as the American Society for Personnel Administration are far from being alone in issuing such warnings.

In 1988, for example, *Business Week* magazine noted that the decline in American birth rates that occurred after 1960 is likely to reduce severely the number of young persons available to take jobs well into the 21st century.

"The years of picky hiring are over," *Business Week* warned. "Vicious competition for all sorts of workers— entry level, skilled, seasonal—has begun. Employers must look to the nonmale, the nonwhite, the nonyoung. . . . Building a new, more diverse workforce and making it tick will be one of corporate America's biggest challenges in the decade ahead."

In 1989 that point was reemphasized when the U.S. Census Bureau projected for the first time that the size of America's population will decline in the 21st century after peaking at about 302 million in the year 2038—even after taking into account existing levels of immigration, legal and illegal. As the post-World War II baby boom ages, the Census Bureau said, the percentage of older persons in the population will rise to the point where, by 2030, nearly one-fourth of the U.S. population will be over age 65.

There are those who argue that America's baby boomers are now beginning to have many babies themselves, and that their offspring will rejuvenate the workforce. But Carl Haub, a demographer with the Population Reference Bureau, refutes that contention. In 1989 the birthrate had risen from an average of 1.9 per woman from its 1976 low of 1.7, but that is still well below the replacement rate of 2.1—and far below the post-war high of 3.7 registered in the mid-1950s.

The Danger of Restriction

In addition to all the evidence that mass immigration could invigorate the American economy, there is empirical evidence that cutting off the flow of hungry-to-work immigrants would be dangerous: It could accelerate the gradual decline of the American economy.

Dr. Thomas Muller, an economist who is highly regarded for his research on the effects of immigration while with The Urban Institute, points out that the Immigration Act of 1924 was one of the factors that caused the depression of the 1930s to be historically a bad one.

"The depression started after immigration was curtailed," Muller points out. "There's no direct cause-and-effect relationship, but one of the causes of the depression was a sharp reduction in demand for housing and consumer goods beginning in about 1926–27. That happened to have coincided with a couple of other things going in that direction.

"Had we maintained immigration at the levels of the early 1920s, which would have been the case had it not been for the Immigration Act of 1924, consumption would have been substantially higher. It would not have prevented the depression, but it would have made it more shallow." Some other countries, such as Canada, didn't legislate against immigration until they were several years into the depression, he points out, and in those countries the efects of the depression were not nearly as severe as in the United States.

Muller's research demonstrates that immigrants generally do not compete with Americans for jobs. Indeed, the entry of low-skilled, hungry-to-work immigrants has often pushed exiting Americans up the employment ladder and improved the quality of life in America.

"When the Chinese came into California, the very unskilled Irish who worked on the railroads—most of whom could neither read nor write—became the crew leaders. The Chinese accepted the bottom level of the work, and the Irish were promoted," Muller points out.

One of the fastest growing job categories in contemporary America is, of course, that of fast-food restaurant workers. The expansion of that occupation is due in large part to the decline of the economic potentials of America's paycheck class: As it becomes increasingly necessary for all adults within a given household to work, the time available for food shopping and cooking at home diminishes. Stretched budgets can't afford fancy restaurants, but fast-food outlets often are an affordable alternative to eating at home.

Low-skilled new immigrants frequently fill the non-managerial jobs in many fast-food operations. Indeed, in Southern California hamburger-chain managers often can be heard directing their all-Hispanic staffs in Spanish.

"The argument could be made 'Well, serve yourself,'" Muller notes, "but that involves a lower quality of life. And that stream of immigrants won't compete with anyone, because we simply don't have the domestic labor for those jobs."

The other major category of contemporary immigrants to America is made up of highly educated people, predominantly Asians.

"Most of them are coming to work in occupations—particularly engineering, scientific and technical positions—where we have a shortage," Muller says. "We are, for a number of reasons, simply not producing sufficient people in those areas. They represent about 20 percent of the immigrant flow. But in some areas, such as the Silicon Valley for example, you'll find that they are about half the workforce."

Even at such high participation levels in lucrative industries, however, immigrants don't consume jobs, they create them. What's more, America's inability to control its borders effectively has allowed the forces of supply and demand to create a nicely balanced flow of immigrants, Muller points out.

"Those at the upper end generate a demand for the others," he says. "An example would be an engineer who earns $70–80,000 per year. That person creates about one and one-half other jobs, because his or her consumption is sufficiently high to create more than one other job. That's the standard multiplier effect for our economy. The more you consume, the more you create work for other people.

"The smaller group on the upper end not only supplies the skills we need—particularly in the context of international competition—but also generates demand for workers at the lower end, which in turn are supplied by a larger group of immigrants.

"If we had only the upper end come in, we'd have a worse situation, because we'd be creating a demand without a supply. On the other hand, if we attracted only the lower end, the economy would slow down technologically. These things all interact."

Muller, who is the author of a forthcoming study of immigration policy underwritten by the prestigious Twentieth Century Fund, has focused much of his most recent research on the effects of immigration on racial and ethnic minorities in America.

"Basically, what we've found," Muller says, "is that there has been no relationship between black unemployment and the flow of Hispanic immigrants. Hispanics tend to be at the lower end of the [economic] spectrum. But if you look at Hispanics, you find no measurable adverse effect [on blacks]." Perhaps that explains why Senator Kennedy's immigration policy staff experiences little pressure from the black community on immigration issues: Although the plight of urban blacks is used as evidence by anti-immigration activists, the blacks themselves perceive no threat from recent immigrants.

In fact, Muller points out, American blacks could benefit from high levels of immigration by low-skill, low-wage groups. "They'd benefit because of their occupational preference," he explains. "Blacks are disproportionately employed in government. If you look at any large city in America, black public-sector employment is very high and it's increasing. Virtually all the net gain in municipal employment in recent years represents black employment."

Most aging urban areas would be declining more rapidly in terms of population if it were not for the flow of low-income immigrants, who tend to move into urban areas as those areas are abandoned by native-born Americans moving to the suburbs and beyond.

"What you have [because of immigration] is an ex-

pansion of population, which creates demand in the
public sector, which then expands black employment
opportunities," Muller says, adding that there is also an
emotional element to the relationship between low-
wage immigrants and blacks: To most contemporary
blacks, working as a cleaning person is a stigmatized
remnant of the times when blacks were held down even
more than today, so becoming a cleaning woman is the
last thing they are willing to do. Many of the new
immigrants now fill the cleaning jobs, allowing black
women to move up, much as the Chinese did for the
Irish in the 19th century.

America's black labor force has raised its skills level
markedly in recent years, Muller notes, and those
blacks who are progressing economically are doing so
rapidly. There is, however, a segment of the black population that is stuck in the urban ghettos, and it is that
group that many people point to in arguing against the
admission of low-skilled immigrants to America.

But in fact, Muller says, that argument is invalid.
"We still have the underclass in the ghettos, and that
seems to be insensitive to immigration or anything else.
It's a different problem, but not one that can be solved
through immigration policy. Limiting immigration is
not going to do anything for that group."

Another ghetto-related argument often made in favor
of immigration restrictions is that impoverished immigrants will put a heavy burden on the welfare system. A
number of studies have discredited that theory, however, and have shown that many contemporary immigrant groups have strong cultural aversions to request-
ing government aid.

The welfare argument against mass immigration is
"probably the weakest," Muller says, but he adds another profound point: The Mexican-Americans who ap-

ply for welfare in the Los Angeles area are largely those who entered America illegally, but whose children are U.S. citizens by virtue of being born in America. The employer sanctions directed at undocumented immigrants that Kennedy and Simpson championed in 1986 prevent many of those parents from working, forcing them to use their children's citizenship to qualify for such welfare programs as Aid to Dependent Children.

"The fact is that periods of great immigration have, without exception, been periods of great expansion, and that expansion has benefited everyone," Muller says. "That's not to say that every individual benefits, or that some individuals are not hurt—as they would be under any conditions. Whenever you have a change in labor force, somebody might not get a job as fast as they would otherwise.

"But from the perspective of the labor force, or from the perspective of the consumer market, or from the perspective of business growth, history tells us that immigration has been one of the major driving forces in the economic expansion of the country from its very origins.

"If, back in the 1790s, limitations had been placed on immigration, our population today would probably be about 60 or 70 million. Despite our natural resources, we essentially would be a second-rate economic influence, at best—like Canada or Australia. It would have been virtually impossible for us to become a major power without immigrant influences."

Formula for Expansion

In addition to the fact that higher immigration results in higher consumption and consequently fuels the economy, one of the most easy-to-understand explanations of why mass immigration causes economic growth exists within the basic economic formula for business expansion. It is a very simple formula that economists typically express in arcane mathematical symbols, thereby boring, confusing and/or alienating noneconomists who need to receive information in conversational terms.

In simple language, the formula for expansion is this: A prudent company will expand as long as the amount of money it gets for producing one more unit of its product is greater than the amount of money that it has to spend to produce that one additional unit. (For those with incurably technical minds, economists express the expansion-encouraging situation as $MR > MC$, marginal revenue is greater than marginal cost. Companies that go bankrupt often seem to be unaware of this formula: By selling a few additional units of their products without regard to the cost of adding an entire second shift of workers or a new line of production machinery, for example, those unprudent companies expand into oblivion.

Apply the formula for prudent expansion to contemporary America and it's easy to see why having employers bid higher and higher wages to attract a shrinking number of available workers isn't the boon to the economy that it seems to be from a paycheck viewpoint. Although wage bidding may seem to create an economic windfall, it quickly brings expansion to a halt: The point at which the cost of one more unit exceeds the money brought in by one more unit is reached more quickly than it would be in a situation where labor was plentiful.

Then a negative chain reaction develops. There is

less work for people who build the commercial build-
ings that expansion would have demanded, for example; building contractors therefore buy fewer trucks,
truck manufacturers buy fewer parts and less steel, and
so on.

This interaction between the cost of labor and the
rate of business expansion has helped create America's
largest, most prosperous cities: New York, Chicago and,
most recently, Los Angeles. Because immigration has at
some point filled those cities with ambitious, inexpensive workers, many companies were established there.
Eventually, groups of companies became industries, the
products they produced became more sophisticated,
and wage scales moved up.

In many parts of contemporary America that same
type of interaction continues to be an essential economic force. While the American auto companies
based in Detroit—a heavily unionized city where workers are conditioned to high hourly rates and extensive
benefit packages—continue to skid down toward ob-
solescence, the Japanese-owned auto companies
gathering in Tennessee—where labor is relatively
cheap, the workers have rejected the unions and there
has always been a shortage of economic opportunities—are booming and expanding.

Labor unions and other jobilists argue that the Japanese automakers are achieving success at the expense
of the working person. But take a look at Detroit, and
then at Nashville, and it's easy to see which is the better
place to be. Then consider the fact that dozens of American and Japanese companies have decided to build
their future plants just south of the Mexican border.
The positive effect that the availability of low-wage
labor has on economic expansion is irrefutable.

Demand vs. Desire

The opposing concept, that of allowing highly educated high-income people to enter America based on their job skills, can sound logical, to be sure. Indeed, it was just such a concept that the provincial Senator McCarran described to his friend Norman Biltz before the senator became infatuated with anti-communism and lost track of his goals for immigration policy. The catch is that already the American economy is proving that highly skilled and educated people are not what it craves.

For example, when the New York State Job Service surveyed employers in the Albany-Schenectady-Troy area in 1989 it found that it was the low-paying positions that were the hardest to fill, while there was an abundance of highly educated and skilled persons for whom there appear to be no openings.

Employers there told the Job Service that they needed to fill 90 amusement-park jobs at an average of $4.80 per hour, but the state could supply only one job candidate. The state also had but one candidate for 24 vegetable-farming jobs at $4.40 an hour. However, one lawyer position paying $8.80 an hour drew 31 applicants, and one writing job paying $14.20 an hour drew 82 job seekers.

What's more, at the time the survey was taken, that region's unemployment rate was at 4.8 percent, less than the level that many economists believe the U.S. labor market can tolerate before giving birth to dangerous levels of inflation.

The contradictions between the perceptions and realities of America's labor market needs raises the issue of the phenomenal amount of expense and expertise that would be required for American government to institute the kind of labor-force central planning that contemporary immigration thinking would require. To even begin to match the flow of immigrants to the workforce by skills and education, the U.S. government would have to create an immense bureaucracy of statistic gatherers, document processors, investigators and the like—something governments have never been able to do efficiently and on time, and without creating huge new opportunities for corruption.

For example, the section of the U.S. Food and Drug Administration that is responsible for monitoring pesticide residues on vegetables routinely takes *six years* to organize and disseminate its findings after picking vegetables for study at random from supermarket shelves.

Immigration officials already have proved their inability to gauge even vaguely the labor needs of the U.S. economy: At the same time that the New York State survey was demonstrating a shortage of amusement park attendants and farm laborers, the INS was routinely handing out a booklet called, oddly enough, *Guide to Immigration Benefits* which stated flatly:

> The administrator has also determined that there are certain occupations for which there are generally sufficient United Sates workers who are able, willing, qualified, and available. . . . Aliens to be employed in such fields . . . should not be encouraged to seek immigration based on such occupations.

The accompanying list of "such occupations" included "amusement and recreational service attendants" and "laborers, farm." Obviously the INS administrator had not consulted with the New York State Job Service before compiling that list.

With that type of mismatching as inspiration, it is easy to imagine hundreds of thousands of the world's most educated and affluent people parading off jetways at airports throughout the United Sates, rejoicing in their long-awaited admission to America—only to find that the jobs for which the government had targeted them had disappeared three years earlier.

Central Planning

The concept of matching immigrants' skills directly to the needs of the U.S. workforce is actually a form of central economic planning. Yet it is the inability of governments to effectively conduct central economic planning of any kind that has caused much of the dissention in communist countries in recent years.

Because communism does not tolerate free markets that regulate production and distribution of goods through the capitalist forces of supply and demand, communist governments typically must decide how much of each product or service will be demanded in any particular region. Often these projections must be attempted many years in advance to allow, for example, a calf to grow into a steer ready for slaughter, or for a grapevine to begin bearing fruit that can be converted into wine that must age for several years before being ready for drinking.

To further illustrate the fallacy of central economic planning, some economists use what is known as the "Parable of the Pencil." Try to plan the production of pencils, they challenge, so that everyone will have enough pencils in the future, but also so that there will never be a surplus of pencils.

First, you'll have to find the kind of land in the correct quantity of acreage to plant enough trees so that forty years later you can harvest the trees for the lumber to form the body of the pencils. At approximately the same time you'll have to find the land to plant a rubber plantation, so that decades later you can harvest the rubber to make the pencil's eraser heads.

You'll also need to develop a schedule of exploration and mining that will supply the metal from which the band that joins the eraser head to the wooden body can be manufactured. And don't forget the exploration and mining for the graphite or "lead" that forms the pencil cores, and for the petroleum that will be required to manufacture the paint with which you'll finish those pencils.

At this point we haven't even begun to consider how much machinery, rolling stock and labor will be required to manufacture and transport the pencils, or the facilities and people that will be needed to distribute them to the populace. But the point is made: It is impossible for any person or organization,let alone government bureaucracies, efficiently to plan economic activity.

Although most Americans don't understand this point, it is the central planning of communist economies, not communism *per se*, that causes all those grocery lines in communist countries that the American news media delight in photographing—and that Americans consider to be one of the best arguments against communism.

Many Americans got a little taste of central planning shock in the 1970s, when President Richard M. Nixon instituted price controls in an attempt to slow inflation. With the forces of supply and demand suspended by government intervention, commodities ranging from sugar to toilet paper soon disappeared from many of America's supermarket shelves as panic buyers acted in anticipation of rumored shortages.

Anyone who has ever traveled via Amtrak, the government-run passenger railroad, has experienced the foibles of central planning as well: There are, inevitably, far too many seats available or far too few.

Despite all the evidence against it, central planning is evolving as America's answer to both immigration policy and labor force needs of the future. Somehow, America is making itself believe that a mechanism that can't effectively manage the supply and demand of a few thousand railroad cars over a period of months can manage the work lives of millions of human beings over five or six decades.

The concept of having the government attempt to match immigrant skills to workforce needs seems even more absurd if one considers the fact that neither jobs nor people are, by any stretch of the imagination, constants.

It is generally accepted among education experts, for example, that the world's rate of technological change in the 1980s was such that, on average, persons in a developed country needed to reeducate themselves approximately every seven years simply to remain competent in their respective occupations. Some occupations change more quickly and some more slowly, of course, but all do change over time.

Since most people in America don't really retire from work at age 65 anymore but continue working well into their '70s, a typical worklife can be expected to span 50 years or more. So even at the contemporary rate of technological change, a rate that logically will accelerate, an individual will need to reeducate himself or herself at least seven times during a worklife.

Do the people who are writing America's job-coordinated immigration laws anticipate tracking each new American immigrant throughout his or her lifetime and ensuring that each accomplishes periodic reeducation? And what of the children of immigrants? Will each new entrant to America be forced to swear that offspring will follow them into their respective occupation and forever maintain competency?

And what if the immigrants or their children switch jobs, as is increasingly necessary as America's economy leaves the stability of the industrial boom times behind? What if the developing crisis in healthcare finance, for example, suddenly diminishes the demand for the nurses who were being admitted to America based on a perceived shortage of nurses? Will America deport anyone who strays from an original work assignment? Would anyone be willing to immigrate to America if such were the case?

If the U.S. government were to declare, as many communist governments have, that it will determine through central planning what each native-born person's life work will be, Americans would revolt. But imposing such regulations on immigrants, it seems, would be acceptable.

Obviously these are concepts which the politicians haven't thought through. With jobilism rampant, they don't need to. All they need to do is to create the *perception* of a rational, politically acceptable approach to immigration policy; by the time the fallacies within that perception have become painfully ·

obvious, people such as Senators Kennedy and Simpson will be sitting back and enjoying their federal pensions.

The trend toward matching immigrant skills to workforce requirements also overlooks the most intangible concept of creativity, which often is described as "luck." "Luck" and "creativity" both have been defined as that spontaneously generated point at which preparation intersects with opportunity. For example, all the musical notes that will ever exist already exist; the process that puts them together into patterns that become "classic" songs that touch previously unrecognized human emotions relies upon the unplannable forces of creativity.

Economic progress also relies heavily on creativity. No one in the 19th century could have anticipated the enormity of the demand that the American economy would one day create for steel or electricity. Yet the new trend in American immigration law, if implemented back then, would have forbidden entry to Andrew Carnegie—who came to America from Scotland to work in a Pittsburgh textile mill, but eventually became the patriarch of the American steel industry. The laws would also have kept out Thomas Alva Edison—a grade-school drop-out who nevertheless invented the first practical incandescent light, as well as the motion-picture projector, the phonograph, and hundreds of other luxuries of modern life.

Like most of the people who climb over and under the fences along America's borders, Carnegie and Edison lacked formal credentials that can be inventoried in a computerized databank. Yet they infused the American economy with the unpredictable-but-necessary forces of creativity. Can you imagine people like those who manage the U.S. Postal Service trying to plan and regulate that?

Diminishing Appeal

Perhaps the most profound long-term flaw, however, in the increasingly popular concept of allowing only the best and brightest to enter America is one rooted in American egocentricity, in the assumption that the cream of the world's work force will *always* choose to move to America—and that America will, consequently, always be in a position of using central economic planning when choosing newcomers for its work force.

Historically, that has not been the case. With the exception of people in the Western Hemisphere who can merely run or swim to America, the bulk of immigration to America has been made up of people who stand slightly above the bottom rung of the economic ladder in their native land. The majority of immigrants coming from any distance have typically been those who could somehow get together the cost of travel but who didn't have very good prospects in their home country. The gap between what their abilities would earn for them at home and what those same abilities would earn for them in America has typically been the primary motivation for immigration to the United States.

Statistics gathered by American business leaders in the '80s show, however, that the difference between economic potentials in America and those in other countries is shrinking, and that the allure of America to potential immigrants may be doing likewise.

For example, the Council on Competitiveness, a

Washington, D.C.-based organization of top-ranked American executives from industry, organized labor and higher eduction, compared the gross national product per capita of all of the world's non-communist countries from 1972 through 1987.

The council uses those figures to gauge relative material standards of living, and it found that although America still was the standard-of-living leader in 1987, the gap between it and the rest of the countries had narrowed considerably during the 15-year period studied, dropping from being 22 pecent higher than the other countries in 1972 to only 9.5 percent higher in 1987. The difference between the United States and Japan had, during that period, narrowed from 48 percent to only 17 percent.

What's more, to maintain even that shrinking standard-of-living gap, the council found, America had relied heavily on foreign capital to finance economic growth. The repayment of that international debt, the council warned, is likely to further diminish the American standard of living.

Consequently, for those highly educated and internationally mobile workers of the future, America may not always be the first choice. Professor LeMay at Frostburg State College points out that as Europe and Japan catch up with the U.S. standard of living, and perhaps surpass it, the world's best and brightest may decide to trust their fate to a more dynamic—and therefore more prosperous—economy. The immense gap that will continue to exist between the affluence levels of even a declining American economy and the economies of Central America and Mexico will long ensure a steady flow of people to relatively nearby America from those areas, despite any attempts to legislate limits to immigration, LeMay points out. And America offers such noneconomic incentives as religious freedom that will continue to attract certain groups of immigrants.

However, other factors coming into play may cause some people wishing to leave other countries to reconsider the choice of America as their immigration objective.

For example, the European Community (known to most Americans as the "Common Market") is working its way toward an easing of economic barriers that have kept its members quite separated in many aspects of business. In doing so, it is creating a mass economy much like that which allowed America to rise to world dominance. At the same time, countries such as West Germany and Great Britian are dealing with immigration much in the same way that America does, but on much smaller scales. Although both of those countries rely on immigrant labor, they consistently legislate against immigration.

"Germany, which has had an official no-immigration policy for decades has had immigration going on for decades. They're trying to cut back from that," LeMay told me in 1989. "The same type of thing is happening in Great Britain. Their policies have been moving in the direction of restriction, but that's going very contrary to the needs their economies are going to have as they unify their economies—especially if that unification brings about the considerable expansion that most economists are predicting.

"Five to ten years from now they may be at the point of desperately needing workers. If that turns out to be the case, the flow might go away from the United States. Two-thirds of the immigration taking place in the world today involves immigration to America, but that may not always be the case.

"The Asian influx to America could even change a bit. Asians who are now clamoring to get into the United States could be clamoring to get into England ten years from now, if the United States of Europe become reality," he said.

"If one can make any safe bet on immigration trends, the safe bet is that they will change. No country has been at the economic and political top of the heap for very long. We are the Rome of the day: The United States has been the number-one world power basically since World War II, so we've enjoyed a half century of that.

"Will we be the major power of the world and will two thirds of all persons who want to migrate always want to migrate to the United States? Ten years from now that's less likely to be the case, maybe dramatically less likely to be the case.

"We may no longer have the (immigration) pressures. Right now we have the pressure of far more people wanting to come in than we can conceivably handle politically," he said.

LeMay notes that he is a political scientist, not an economist, and is therefore not in a position to prescribe an upper limit for mass immigration. But he argues that America could easily accommodate at least twice as many immigrants per year as it currently accepts.

"We could probably easily absorb double what we legally allow," he said. "We could have a million immigrants coming in a year and we'd handle them swimmingly. There would be some social pressures, cultural pressures, but in the long run we'd benefit from it."

Throwing Down One Piece

It must be noted that there was one politician in America of the 1980s who was willing to stand fearlessly and take an iconoclastic position in support of the economic contributions of immigrants. Ironically, he is from McCarran's home state of Nevada and he was, at this writing, only a state assemblyman. But in 1989 he did something that is likely to affect America's racial and ethnic image of itself for generations to come.

On May 11, 1989, Representative Wendell P. Williams introduced in the Nevada Legislature Assembly Bill 759 which simply amends an existing law that gives the state board of education the right to chose textbooks to be used in Nevada's public schools. The new language that he proposed is, however, profound in its simplicity:

> A textbook may not be selected for use in the public schools in classes in literature, history, or social sciences unless it accurately portrays the cultural and racial diversity of our society, including lessons on the contributions made to our society by men and women from various racial and ethnic backgrounds.

Editorial writers scoffed at Williams's proposal, and political critics called it grandstanding, but his concept touched a special nerve that runs through all of America and support for his amendment began to snowball. The Nevada State Education Association endorsed it, as did the Clark County School District and Nevada's state superintendent of schools.

In response to an editorial criticizing his bill, Williams wrote a rebuttal that depicted America's various racial and ethnic groups metaphorically as members of a team in a relay race: "Americans of color are not another team in competition with America. If America keeps running without the baton, no matter how fast or how far, we're all going to lose. Young people with skills and abilities are all our children. And until they can sing 'This land is your land, this land is my land,' and that's a fact, we, America, will not thrive at the level of our potential."

The unexpected support that swelled up behind Williams's proposal reminded me of a philosophy expressed by Father Langford during one of our conversations in the yard of his mission in Murua. Controversies such as those surrounding immigration to America can sometimes seem so complex, Langford pointed out, that intellectual paralysis sets in: There seems to be no simple solution, so why do anything?

The philosophy that Langford espouses says, in contrast, that no one person must come up with a complete solution. Each person must do what he or she believes to be right, even though that action alone may not seem to bring about a resolution of the problem. "You have to throw down the first piece of the puzzle," Langford said, "and sometimes you feel stupid standing there with your one piece. But you have to believe that the other pieces will come along."

Williams threw down his piece of America's immigration puzzle and some people did, indeed, attempt to make him look stupid. But the other pieces soon began, as Langford's philosophy promises, to fall in place. At this writing his proposal had received unanimous approval in the Nevada Senate and was sitting on the governor's desk for approval. Educators in other states were beginning to inquire about the new law with thoughts of putting similar requirements into effect within their jurisdictions.

Perhaps America doesn't need *all* the would-be immigrants who exist on earth; indeed, no one really knows how many there are or how many could even afford to make the trip. On the other hand no one has been able to prescribe a scientifically formulated *upper limit* for immigration to America. What the evidence shows is simply that America needs all the immigrants *it can get*, and that opening America's borders to everyone but known criminals and people with incurably contagious diseases would enhance the country's level of prosperity.

What's more, the public reaction to Representative Williams's initiative shows that, freed from the assumptions of the self-perpetuating immigration bureaucracy, most Americans would welcome the opportunity to participate in a meritocracy in which everyone has an even chance to succeed.

Do the arguments in favor of mass immigration treat people as a commodity, as the National Council of La Raza argues? Maybe so, but discussing immigrants as a commodity is the candid and honest way to discuss the role that immigrants truly play in the success of the American economy. Romanticism aside, neither the science of economics nor the people who own and manage businesses can calculate the people factor in any way other than as a commodity; indeed, modern economists and managers regard people as the most *essential* commodity.

That fact clashes with the romantic notions with which America's paycheck class regards itself. Just as most people would cringe at the seemingly cold terms physicians and clergymen use to discuss their patients and parishioners when talking with colleagues behind closed doors, paycheck-class Americans would be shocked to see that they are represented as mathematical digits and dollars signs on corporate management reports.

It is, however, very important to note that although the Irish who were herded into the steerage of ships bound for America to serve as ballast were most definitely regarded as a commodity, that fact didn't prevent one of their progeny from becoming the most revered American president of the 20th century.

Despite all this evidence in favor of open immigration, there are two arguments that have most often been raised against open immigration—and which will, without a doubt, continue to be raised.

The oldest, dating back to at least the 19th century, is that there is no more room left in America for more people. The second, a child of the world's transition from the Industrial Era to the Information Age, is that the people who want to come to America wouldn't be able to do the increasingly technological work that America needs to have done.

So in the next two chapters let's examine those two arguments to see whether they really counterbalance all the evidence of America's continuing need for immigrant workers of all levels.

CHAPTER 7

The Question of Space and Location

S IMPLY BY BROWSING the headlines in a typical American newspaper, it is easy to develop the frequently heard opinion that there is no more room left in America—that no one else should be allowed to immigrate because those people who are already living in the United States are being squeezed up against one another with increasing frequency.

Take, for example, the story of Larry Fuller, a carpenter from Tioga, West Virginia, who decided in 1989 to move to Washington, D.C., in search of better employment opportunities. A shortage of labor already existed in America's capital, so within hours of his arrival the 25-year-old Fuller was hired for an $8-per-hour job with an electric utility company.

Things were looking up until he discovered that a person making $8 an hour can't afford to live in Washington, D.C. The migration of money and hordes of people from throughout the United States to the nation's capital had driven prices and apartment rents

204

there to extraordinary heights. For weeks Fuller had to live in a campground while searching for affordable housing. "Back in Tioga I could live in a palace and have money left over on what I make here," he told a reporter for the *New York Times*.

But in Washington, D.C., he could afford only a pup tent and he was, at the time the news media discovered him and a number of others in similar situations, thinking of moving back home.

His problems and those of the millions who spend a substantial portion of their time sitting in their cars in the traffic jams that encircle most American cities, or searching for a home—any home—they can afford, appear to indicate that America should hang out a "no vacancy" sign. But if that's true, then how does one explain the problems of places such as Koochicing County, Minn., which made headlines in 1988 by offering to give up to 40 acres of land to anyone who would build a house on the land and live in it for at least ten years?

"The population's dropping and that hurts the schools, the power company, everything," one Koochicing County resident told reporters after the free land offer was made public. "If we don't get neighbors, we won't be able to live here, either."

As the concerns of places such as Koochicing County imply, America hasn't *really* run out of places in which people can find a home. The congestion and costliness of the urban areas may make it seem as though that's the case, but in fact America's problems with congestion have no connection with the rate of immigration. Even if immigration were to stop completely, the tendency of the majority of Americans to trip over one another would continue to grow.

According to studies conducted in the late 1980s by

the U.S. Census Bureau, about 50 percent of all Americans live in just 37 metropolitan areas, yet about 90 percent of all population growth—from both native-born and immigrant sources—in America was taking place in and around metropolitan areas.

There are many factors that contribute to this proclivity for urban congestion. Advances in the technology of agriculture in the second half of the 20th century, for example, have greatly diminished the number of attractive economic opportunities in farming, leaving former rural residents no option but to move toward the cities. Some studies have also shown that, pronouncements to the contrary notwithstanding, the chief executive officers of American corporations most often relocate corporate headquarters not to the most advantageous and efficient location, but to an area close to home in their favorite metropolis, dragging their company's work force behind them.

Other studies have shown that defense spending by the U.S. government—which is distributed on the basis of political impact and, therefore, is directed disproportionately to areas with the largest number of voters—greatly reinforces the syndrome of increasing employment in and around the most crowded cities.

The growth of government as a percentage of the America's gross national product has had a great influence on the trend toward metropolitan congestion as well. Partly as a result of the payroll tax-withholding concept that was instituted during the development of the country's postwar paycheck-based culture, nearly one in every three dollars spent in America was being spent by government in the late 1980s. Consequently, Washington, D.C., and the capitals of virtually every state in the union became increasingly high-priced and crowded as people migrated there from the areas from which the tax dollars had been drained.

For instance, the average after-tax household income in the Washington, D.C., area rose from the already lofty level of 32 percent above the national average in 1980 to 48 percent above the national average in 1988. Washington housing prices inflated accordingly during those eight years, and people like Larry Fuller who migrated from less tax-rich areas were left living in pup tents.

The factor that looms largest in America's continuing excursion into metropolitan congestion, however, is the country's unique approach to the geography of business and work. Unlike other industrialized economies such as those of Japan and Europe, the American economy has always been land rich. Consequently, America developed a unique approach to industrial siting, and that created the sprawling suburbs. And the suburbs are, of course, where the Olympic-level traffic jams and the breathtaking housing-price escalations that infuriate contemporary Americans were born.

Fading Geospecifics

At the start of the Industrial Revolution, American businesses had to remain located near oceans, rivers and the Great Lakes in order to transport their goods efficiently. In the 19th century, railroads began providing a viable alternative to water transport and opened up huge new geographic regions to economic development. As America moved into the 20th century, trucks and highways further enhanced the ability of industry to locate in a variety of places, because factories and warehouses no longer needed to be located along a waterfront or rail line.

Jet aircraft made frequent travel and freight transport by air convenient in the 1960s, and by the mid 1980s it was possible to conduct business in virtually any city in America and have the results arrive the next morning in any other city via one of several air-express services.

At the same time, the nature of what America produces was changing. American companies became increasingly involved in the processing of information, and information is a commodity that doesn't need a railroad boxcar or tractor-trailer truck to move it around.

The tangible things that human beings and businesses utilize in everyday activities have become much lighter in the latter half of the 20th century as well. Plastics and featherweight fibers have replaced cast iron and steel in many applications, for example. Even within the computer industry, tiny, virtually weightless microchips have replaced big-and-bulky vacuum tubes over just a few decades.

What's more, the geographic requirements of much of the world's commerce were nearly obliterated in 1989, when fiber-optic communication cables laid across the floors of both the Atlantic and Pacific oceans went into service—thereby allowing the products of information processing to flow at the speed of light among Europe, America and Asia.

Lagging Behind Technology

People do not change as rapidly, however, as the technologies they create. And therein lies the explanation for most of the traffic jams, the housing "shortages," and all the stresses generated by the congestion of America's cities that seem to point to a need to restrict immigration.

Although the needs of most commerce to be located on a bay or river has disappeared, most of America's largest commercial hubs remain where they were back before the introduction of land- and air-based transportation. Instead of taking bold steps inland to the places where land is so abundant that the government has to pay farmers to stop growing food on it, American corporations and the people who work in them have merely tiptoed out from their original homes, forming rings of economic nodules that surround the urban ports and train depots that supported the adolescence of the Industrial Revolution in the 19th century.

Most of those nodules were formed through an unintended leap-frogging effect that started with a trickle of wealthy people into the countryside as the new factories drew newly arrived immigrants and former farmers into urban manufacturing areas in the late 19th century. The formation of the "suburbs" accelerated, however, as automobiles became affordable to the average American family during the country's post-World War II economic boom. The automobile made it possible for America's then-growing middle class to begin moving out of the cramped old cities and into the suburbs, where they could comfortably maintain three children, a lawn, a garage and even a dog. The era of the "commuter" was born.

In 1956, President Dwight D. Eisenhower signed into law a program to create 41,000 miles of limited-access interstate highways designed to handle traffic traveling at up to 75 miles per hour. Those highways would, he hoped, allow American troops to move as quickly through the U.S. countryside as he had seen them move through rural Germany on the autobahns during his days as a World War II combat commander. But provincial political deals and concessions to the then-powerful construction trade unions pulled the interstate routes in close to America's cities, and what eventually was built bore little resemblance to the autobahns. It became, instead, a national system of metropolitan beltways with entry and exit ramps for each substantial suburban community.

Soon, some city-based companies found that they could find plenty of cheap workers and cheap land out in the newly accessible suburbs, and that some workers, particularly the former housewives who were beginning to enter the work force, would even accept lower pay if they didn't have to get dressed up and commute into the central city each day. Some companies also found that they could speed up their assembly lines if they built them all on one level; with land in the suburbs available at relatively cheap prices, why not? So those companies moved a few miles out into the suburbs, too. Subsequently, the growing availability of work in the suburbs attracted even more workers out of the cities.

Suburban land and home prices began to rise with the arrival of the new workers. Exacerbated by the inflation of the '60s and '70s, the rising housing prices in the suburbs seemed to be a trend that would never end, so the huge wave of baby boomers who were entering adulthood and the work force in those decades began to speculate up housing prices dramatically.

Then some workers at those suburban companies discovered that by moving just a little bit farther out they could cut their housing costs or afford a larger house—or even a small farmette on which to keep the horse that they suddenly found they could afford for the kids. Other companies followed those workers out to the "exurbs," which then evolved into still more suburbs, and so on.

Eventually the suburbs and exurbs of land-rich America began to blur into "metropolitan areas." For example, the entire state of New Jersey—which still calls itself "The Garden State" and as late as the 1960s supported substantial levels of commercial farming—is now regarded by Census Bureau statisticians as a metropolitan area because of the congestion it has developed as an outrigger of New York City. And yet by driving less than 100 miles west from New Jersey's border with Pennsylvania, one encounters vast woodlands so isolated from urbanity that it is difficult to tune a station in on the car radio.

Despite the relative decentralization of urban economies out of central cores and into the nearby suburbs, however, American business often hangs on to the extremely centralized concept of work created within the crudely managed factories of the late 19th century. The New York and American stock exchanges provide a good example: They could have followed the lead of America's NASDAQ Exchange and the stock exchanges of some other countries many years before by having all trading take place within computer networks. But in the late 1980s the New York and American stock exchanges were still employing human beings to stand on the exchange floors in the centuries-old financial district located adjacent to New York Harbor's oldest piers and execute trades.

Consequently, hundreds of floor brokers and the thousands of "back office" clerical personnel needed to support the brokers' efforts throng into the streets of New York's financial district after a long ride from the suburbs each day, cursing and bitching about the congestion, to do work that could just as well be performed by a computer situated on what used to be a corn field in Iowa. Despite the decentralization of commerce, the

centralization of work is a habit that America finds
hard to kick.

Traversing the Nodules

One of the most expert observers of this syndrome is
Dick Netzer, former dean of the School of Public Administration at New York University, author of several
books on urban economics, and now Senior Fellow at
NYU's Urban Research Center in Manhattan. To use
America's growing metropolitan congestion as an argument against immigration, he says, is simply "absurd."

Most of the people who find themselves virtually
parked for hours each day on the superhighways and
expressways that ring the metropolitan areas where
most of America's work is done, he points out, are not
battling burgeoning masses of urban population but are
merely driving between and within all those outrigger
suburban business nodules. And, unlike the days when
people commuted by foot, trolley, bus, ferry or train to
relatively nearby central business districts, the auto-
mated scramble in the suburbs often has no dominant
directional flow.

"What's happening in every large metropolitan area
of the United States, and even in some that are not so
large, is that the cities are becoming what is known in
the jargon of the economics trade as 'multi-nucleated',"
Netzer says. "There are big nodes of employment outside the city. The people who continue to commute
into central cities find that the commutes are getting
longer, partly because they make those choices. But the
other thing that is true in all large metropolitan areas is
that trips have become harder because congestion
within the suburbs—not going to and from the central
city—has become so horrendous.

"Anybody who is going from one of the outer suburbs to the city centers has to traverse that. It's everywhere, and it's the largest transportation problem this country has, and frankly no one has the slightest idea what to do about it. But it's definitely not a problem related to immigration," he says.

Netzer points to the San Bernardino freeway that runs east and west through the heart of Los Angeles as the worst of the worst among America's congestion problems, and a strong example of the suburban leap-frogging principle. Because of rampant speculation in the Southern California residential housing market, many younger families moved into the high desert— euphemistically known as "The Inland Empire"—east of Lost Angeles during the '80s to purchase relatively low-priced tract homes that they hope will appreciate in price as well.

"In the middle of the day, from San Bernardino all the way into the Los Angeles central business district, you can have traffic moving at 10 to 15 miles per hour," Netzer says. "That's not commuting, that's suburban congestion. That was not a problem in the old central cities because there enough of it was handled by public transportation and walking, not just for getting to and from work but for all sorts of trips."

Conversely, some of America's older and inherently more efficient central urban areas have been rescued by recent immigrants, Netzer points out. Because the less-affluent immigrants often are willing to accept older, less-verdant housing situations, immigrants have prevented many of America's older cities from declining into abandonment as native-born people move out into the tree-lawned suburban morass in search of better employment opportunities and house-price profits.

"We have room in all those areas—because most central cities have smaller populations now than they had at one time," he says. "That's not so true of Los Angeles or Houston or Dallas or Phoenix, but it is true of the older cities of the United States. You can have economic growth just by in-filling, and in some cities that's beginning to happen.

"In New York we have spectacular examples of immigrants moving into older neighborhoods—neighborhoods that might have become declining neighborhoods. They've been rescued by immigrants."

If companies were to decide that, instead of building new facilities in the metropolitan suburbs or in the *maquiladora* developments, they will locate their new facilities in the many uncrowded parts of America that are begging for people and commerce, many immigrant groups would be willing to move to those new locales. Indeed, the history of the populating of America is dominated by the dispersion of immigrants to economic opportunities wherever they existed.

If such dispersion were to begin again, prosperous new American cities would be created and the pressure of congestion that spreading economic development puts on the suburbs that surround the 19th century business hubs would be reduced. But politics and America's tradition of immigrant rivalries prohibit that, Netzer predicts.

"Any company that proposed to do that would be quickly advised by everybody under the sun that it was going to take on substantial additional responsibilities. It would become a political problem: The host community would say 'Ok, then you provide health care facilities,' for example, and all sorts of other things that were not provided for these kinds of people in the 19th century," he says.

"If it were a small-scale thing—attracting say 150

immigrants to an older Midwestern city, for example—nothing would happen. But if you were to say 'We and several other firms are going to do this and possibly attract 7,000 people to a place where the work force is perhaps 40,000,' you would run into a lot of social and political objections.

"But it would create a boomtown. It makes a great deal of sense from a standpoint of national policy to say that, for immigrants who have no particular reason to stay in metropolitan areas, we're going to have supporting mechanisms for them to move into the less densely populated sections of the country. A lot of Laotians would be better off, a lot of Central Americans would be better off, this country probably would be better off," he says.

Another potential barrier to redistributing American commerce and the work force away from urban sprawl, Netzer explains, is the fact that many of America's contemporary immigrants are accustomed to climates more temperate than those existing in many of the wide-open areas of the United States. "But the climate thing may not be as big a problem as we think," Netzer says, pointing out the fact that Canada gets a surprising number of immigrants from the relatively warm-climate country of India.

To reinforce this point, Netzer cites an anecdote he picked up through his hobby interest in the Arctic. "I heard of a man who came to Canada as an immigrant from Madras, India," he recalls. "He was really poor and didn't have much money or much in the way of skills, and the only job he could get was in the Arctic. He went up to the Arctic and worked there, and eventually became the owner of a small hotel and the operator of trips in the high Arctic. He married an Eskimo woman and lives in the Eskimo settlement

called Resolute, which is about 75 degrees north lati-
tude. I'm an Arctic freak, so you can believe me that it's
not warm there."

Congestion Cures Itself

At some point America may begin to utilize energetically the technologies of the late 20th century to alleviate some of the situations that make the country appear
to have run out of room for people. Some industries
have already done so in small ways: Several airlines
utilized improved telecommunications capabilities in
the 1980s, for example, to move their reservation-proc-
essing operations away from the crowded coasts and
into smaller, inland cities.

Eric H. Monkkonen, a professor of history at the
University of California, Los Angeles who specializes
in urban trends and author of *America Becomes Urban*
(University of California Press, 1988), points out that
this kind of thinking may become more common because congestion typically forces people and organizations to rethink their habits and situations in a constructive way.

"One of the solutions to congestion is congestion
itself," he says. "If people are really spending too much
time driving on freeways, then they'll move. The U.S.
population has always been mobile, and one of the
things that we know is happening is that business is
moving.

"Why are people living too far from work? Because
they want lower housing prices, or whatever. It's a
trade-off. The solution to the problem is for people to
move to smaller places."

Some of the new technologies of work, such as fac-
simile transmission machines and computer modems,

may help businesses to do just that—to disperse throughout the United States in the 21st century as they did in the 19th. Manufacturing operations are likely to continue to require teams of people to gather under one roof, Monkkonen points out, but with the acceptance of new technologies that roof can be built over ground that is far from the congested metropolitan area.

Meanwhile, however, congestion befuddles many Americans, and forces them to seek a simple factor such as immigration on which to blame it. "The reason for these feelings is that, as cities and the immigrant groups change, one often sees an old neighborhood that used to be low-density become high-density, and that seems awful," Monkkonen says. "But there's plenty of room in places such as central Detroit, and that's equally irrational."

The Perception of Emptiness

Has American run out of room for new immigrants? Obviously, the answer is an overwhelming "no." Researchers have generated a continual flow of interesting illuminations of this point, such as the fact that every person on earth could be put into the state of Texas and the density there would still be less than in some existing cities.

Julian L. Simon, professor of economics at the University of Maryland and author of many of the leading texts on population theory, has estimated that less than 3 percent of the land area of the United States is occupied by urban areas. America is not running out of resources as the headlines indicate, Simon often points out, but is merely in the process of discovering and adopting new and more efficient ways of utilizing its resources. Consider, for example, the lack of progress in the improvement of the efficiency of the typical American toilet: Although many parts of the United States suffer from chronic water-supply shortages, the people who live in those regions routinely excrete a few ounces of urine into several *gallons* of treated drinking water, which must shortly thereafter be recleaned in an expensive-to-operate treatment plant.

Other economists, such as Professor McKenzie at Clemson, stress the possibility that new technologies may succeed in obliterating the geospecifics of work on earth without ever stopping to correct the geographic errors of America's slow-to-change corporations. Instead of moving jobs the short distance from the central city areas to the suburbs in search of affordable labor, they point out, aggressive companies are increasingly transferring nonmanagerial work directly from the cores of U.S. cities to faraway *countries* and managing the work from America's suburbs via telephone and computer modem.

But perhaps the most succinct retort to the contention that America does not have the room and resources within it to accept and support new waves of mass immigration comes from Dr. Jacqueline Kasun, professor of economics at Humboldt State University in Arcata, California. In her book *The War Against Population* (Ignatius Press, 1988), she points out that when pondering the amount of space left for people in the United States, "The feeling of the typical air passenger that he is looking down on a mostly empty earth is correct."

CHAPTER 8

The Question of Education and Training

IMAGINE FOR A MOMENT the fate of this troubled work force of the year 2000, described in a commentary written for *U.S. News & World Report* by Marian Wright Edelman, president of the Children's Defense Fund:

"One in four of them is poor. For black kids, one in two is poor. One is six hasn't got any health insurance. One in two has got a mother in the labor force and is not getting decent child care. One in five is going to be a teen parent. One in seven is going to drop out of school. This is a recipe for a national catastrophe."

Edelman was describing not the future work force of an impoverished, undeveloped Third World country but that of the United States. And shortly after she made that assessment a report from the U.S. Department of Education showed that the decline Edelman was predicting had already begun.

The study followed 25,000 American high school graduates through the 1980s, and it found that students who completed high school in 1982 had gained post-secondary degrees at a rate less than half that of those who had finished high school in 1972. That report was "enormous by any social standard," Vincent Tinto, a professor of education at Syracuse University told the *Wall Street Journal.* "We're running the risk of having a more bipolar, stratified society than we have now."

It is becoming painfully obvious that the legacy of America's industrial boom period does not include a net increase in intellectual prowess or even social so-phistication. Indeed, to many of these Americans who can remember their immigrant parents' or grand-parents' energetic discussions of world history, politi-cal and social issues around the family dinner table, a net decline in the average level of sophistication in America is readily apparent—even without the il-lumination of formal reports on the trend.

When I talk before American groups in connection with my writing on employment-related issues, I often find that the most sophisticated questions and com-ments afterward come from teenage exchange students from Europe and Asia. Many of the American-born adults in the audience, on the other hand, seem not to understand even the most basic concepts underlying the employment relationship. For many of the latter, of course, success in America's post-World War II indus-trial boom times required only the punching of the timeclock and the paying of union dues.

The gap between the intellectual level of the typical American and the typical citizen of other developed countries was made particularly obvious in the late 1980s by an international student exchange program. Students from other countries were invited to tell their

American peers about their homelands as part of World Awareness Week.

Ben Ko, then a 20-year-old student visiting from Korea as part of that program, expressed to *The Denver Post* his dismay at the fact that the American students with whom he spoke were not only unable to find his native country on a map, they were also unfamiliar with the geography of their own country. "When I was in L.A., I would say 'I'm from Denver'," he said. "And they would say, 'Where's that? Near Washington, D.C.?'"

Some people have actually built businesses upon the exploitation of America's lack of sophistication. One of the most prominent newspaper management consultants of the 1980s, for example, once was quoted as advising American publishers to dumb-down their products because, he said, America is a country "where half the people are driving around with phony rubber dice hanging from their windshield."

The Universal Challenge

The challenge of matching the skills and education of the American work force to that of the 21st-century economy is not, therefore, one that is specific to newly arriving immigrants. Indeed, the hard truth is that if American citizenships were awarded competitively based on intellectual development instead of birthright, a large percentage of native-born Americans would find themselves living on the southern bank of the Rio Grande.

How did this happen? Why did rising material affluence not translate into ever-higher levels of education, intellectualism and marketable skills for the average American?

There has been much debate over what to do about the future of education and training in America, and hundreds of amazingly simplistic quick-fixes have been suggested. In 1989, for example, educators in West Virginia put forward a plan to revoke the automobile driver's license of any student who drops out of school. At the same time another educational group suggested that the problem could be resolved by subjecting teachers to more complex forms of professional licensing—a concept that, history shows, has never guaranteed or increased competence in any profession.

Very little has been said, however, about how the American work force worked its way down the intellectual ladder. But clues abound in a variety of places and situations. Ironically, one of the most explicit parallels can be found in many of the maquiladoras along the Mexican-American border.

When the Rev. Justice Worth, a Franciscan priest, visited some of the maquiladoras in 1989 he found that many Mexican teenagers were ignoring formal education so that they could work in the factories. As a reaction to the mind-numbing work they did, many of them were becoming involved with drugs. Even though the factories pay only a few dollars for a full day of monotonous manual labor, the compensation seems large to impoverished Mexican teenagers. In some towns, Father Worth reported in an article for the National Catholic Reporter, only one or two percent of the teenagers complete high school.

"In five or ten years we will have the problem," a local parish priest told him. "These youth will be burnt out from the monotonous work, and will have nowhere to go. They will have no education to build upon."

Even as America entered the 1990s, a similar syndrome was exerting its influence among the employees of the rapidly expanding Japanese-owned auto plants in Tennessee. When the United Auto Workers union launched an all-out but unsuccessful campaign to organize the workers of a Nissan plant just outside Nashville, many of those workers publicly expressed the fact that all they wanted from life was to have the plant that employed them continue to employ them for the rest of their lives.

Many of those Nissan workers were only in their 20s or 30s. They had been born and raised in America, where education through high school costs the individual nothing, and virtually anyone can go through a trade school or two-year college on a government grant or loan, and then pursue something more than a lifetime of production-line laboring. But relative to the other wage-working situations they had seen in their relatively impoverished hometowns, they felt the Nissan wage rates were wildly generous. Having not seen the other side of the mountain through education, they were content merely to drive bolts and lift mufflers for the rest of their lives. "This is as good as it gets," one Nissan worker gushed to reporters.

The Price of High Wages

America and other industrialized countries have experienced this trade-off between relatively high-paying manual labor and education even since it became temporarily possible during the post-World War II years to earn a comfortable income through little more than manual labor.

Management expert Peter F. Drucker addressed this well in his book *The New Realities* (Harper & Row, 1989), which analyzed many of the issues that are accompanying the industrialized world into the 21st century. During the post-war industrial boom times, he points out, the economic incentives operated in direct opposition to an emphasis on learning.

"Even in the decades following World War II when college enrollments exploded and knowledge rapidly became the economy's foundation and true 'capital,' the quickest and easiest road to a good job and job security in developed countries was not through education," he observed. "It was going at age seventeen into a unionized mass-production factory as a semiskilled worker. A year later, often sooner, that worker earned more in all developed countries (excepting only Japan) than the holder of the university degree could expect to earn for fifteen or twenty years."

Only in mass-market America, however, did high-paying manual labor attract such huge numbers of people that wage-working became the very soul of the national culture, at the expense of intellectual development. And it is within the results of these circumstances that contemporary labor market economists find the need to better coordinate the skills of the American work force to the higher-level skills required by the economy of the 1990s and beyond.

Reports such as *Workforce 2000* are not saying, as contemporary immigration-law proposals simplistically imply, that America must allow only the most highly skilled and educated persons to enter. What the studies are saying is that America needs more workers than it can produce through indigenous reproduction—and that everyone who goes to work in America, immigrant or native born, will have to take an aggressive approach to work-related learning as the world moves into the 21st century.

This concept is so widely misunderstood that it even generated a hint of class warfare during the presidential election of 1988. Candidate George Bush, whose public image is so aristocratic and New England-ish that many Americans have forgotten that he's a Texan, told a group of students at Garfield High School in Los Angeles: "You don't have to go to college to be a success. . . . We need the people who run the offices, the people who do the hard physical work of our society."

Shortly thereafter, candidate Jesse Jackson, whose political appeal is built upon his proletarian affiliations with the late Martin Luther King, Jr., issued a retort to Bush while speaking before a group at Hampton University in Virginia. "Let *him* caddy. Let *him* shine shoes. *You* keep going to college," Jackson bellowed.

Room in the Middle

Actually, President Bush came closer to the essential point in that exchange. A report released in 1989 by the Center for Continuing Study of the California Economy illustrates this well.

"There will be plenty of new jobs in the middle level," notes the report in a section on future employment opportunities. "People do not have to jump from low-skilled work to professional status. The middle is alive and well.

"But the middle is changing. . . . Most jobs are people related and involve work in offices, stores and the health and education sectors. The issue is one of balance—whether the number of low-skilled workers is equal to or in excess of the economy's requirements."

The key factor in maintaining that balance, the report says, is upward mobility.

"Upward movement is vital for two reasons:

"1.) There is a limited amount of room at the bottom of the occupational structure—only so many low-skilled jobs are needed. If the new immigrants are to take many of the low-skilled jobs, the previous generation must 'move on' which means 'move up.'

"2.) At the same time, the 'upward movement' of the previous generation of less-skilled labor force entrants (immigrant or not) is the only way for the state's labor force to make the upward occupation shift needed to keep pace with the needs of the California economic base.

"The potential problem of a mismatch between the skills of the future labor force and the requirements of tomorrow's economy is not confined to California. It is a national issue. There are two principal long-term strategies that are emerging in response to these issues. One strategy involves training and education for the adult population already in the labor force.

"The other strategy involves focusing the nation's educational systems on improving the success rate and providing quality education to people who are 'falling through the cracks.' Both strategies are finding support in the private sector as well as public sector policy arenas. . . . The principal long-term strategy is to strengthen the education system of the state and nation."

Time magazine made a similar point in a 1989 report on what it called "The Forgotten Half" of America's developing workforce. "Stereotypes of noncollege-bound youth as janitors or hamburger flippers have fed the notion that Americans who lack a college degree are economically inconsequential," Time observed. "in fact, half of all young American workers still do not attend college. And in the upcoming decade, the economy will depend as much on this diverse group of less schooled workers as it will on the nation's software programmers and rocket scientists."

Obviously, the same facts apply to incoming immigrants. To allow in only those with prestigious college degrees and highly specialized skills would ignore at least half of the needs of the American economy. What's worse, limiting the right to immigrate to only the best and brightest would put a substantial portion of the native-born American work force—particularly those millions of Americans whose only educational edge over impoverished immigrants is the ability to speak English—in the position of having an immigrant, often one of a different race, as their boss. That would be a situation which, history shows, could only create new and potentially dangerous levels of immigrant rivalries.

Paying the Bill

Although it is frequently confused with credentialism in America, education in the context of work force issues is generally defined as the teaching of foundation concepts and skills, such as the ability to read, write and perform arithmetic. The teaching of occupation-specific abilities is generally referred to as "training." The absence of either one greatly diminishes the value of the other, so the American work force of the '90s and beyond needs both. But who will bear the financial burden of educating and training the new American work force, both immigrant and native born?

Government has already proved that it is unable to provide in a sincere and honest way the education and training that the work force of the future needs. The shortcomings of the public education system have been widely documented so they need not be repeated here. And just as many millions of dollars as in housing funds that were supposed to aid the poor ended up in the pockets of wealthy real estate developers and their political allies in the 1980s, government money intended to train Americans for the jobs of the 1990s and beyond has most often gone to shady business people who know how to play the political system.

Rather than serving as a foundation for America's future, the government's efforts at employment-related training have served as little more than bi-partisan pork-barrels. For example, in reviewing the results of the 1983 Job Training and Partnership Act (JTPA) sponsored by Vice-President Dan Quayle, then a Senator from Indiana, and Senator Edward Kennedy, the General Accounting Office found that about 43 percent of the contracts that the JTPA bureaucracy made with private employers who were supposed to be training workers were for such low-skill occupations as custodians and dishwashers—jobs that many of the immigrants being kept out of America could and would do with no training.

"In many instances, on-the-job training contracts appeared to provide wage subsidies to employers," the GAO said in 1989. "School dropouts were underserved and received little remedial education."

One of the most outspoken advocates for a rethinking of America's attitude toward the development of a work force for the 21st century is David D. Hale, chief economist for the Chicago-based Kemper Financial Services Inc. Hale, who often testifies on national economic issues before various congressional committees, began advocating increased levels of both immigration and work force training in the late 1980s.

It is difficult to correlate the cost of educating and training workers to their individual contributions to the American economy, Hale points out, because individuals vary so greatly. But America does need a mix of people to fill all the vacant slots that are developing in the country's work force, he says. In the late 1980s, for example, Boston was experiencing a severe labor shortage despite the high number of highly educated immigrants living there, while cities in the American Southwest were having fewer problems with labor shortages because of their proximity to impoverished Mexico.

"There's no reason to restrict immigration to highly educated people, but if you're going to allow in badly educated people, you're going to have to have an educational structure to absorb them. This is a particularly important problem for America because of the nature of our population," Hale told me in 1989.

"We have a large unskilled and semi-skilled population in the United States. Meanwhile, the job requirements for operating in this society are getting more and demanding because of technology and machinery.It's very clear that sheer brawn won't be enough any more.

"The populations of Japan, of Sweden, or of Holland are very homogeneous, they're 99 percent literate. They have a kith-and-kin kind of camaraderie where social institutions and the private sector interact with the public sector in ways that tend to guarantee that no one falls through the cracks. When you have a racially heterogeneous society as America has, however, a lot of people fall through the cracks. Some groups don't feel any obligation to other groups."

Hale believes that America's business community will have to bear the brunt of the cost of training the work force of the future, even though that will result in a sort of double taxation, since industry already pays much of the bill for the public education system. But the price must be paid, and the key to making all those expenditures productive and efficient is to coordinate America's educational system more closely to the actual skill needs of the economy—instead of relying on obsolete public-school rituals and the drive to make corrupt profit from the politicization of government training programs.

"First, I'd establish criteria for what we're actually doing, and what we're getting in the way of productivity," he said. "Then, because of the way our system is organized you can't bypass state and local governments, so you'd have to find some way to work with them."

Luckily some segments of American industry are already following Hale's advice. Some large employers are demanding that they be given the right to help guide the public education system in return for the money they contribute to that system through both taxes and grants.

"The public schools don't work worth a damn," Joseph F. Alibrandi, chief executive of Whittaker Corporation in Los Angeles told *The Wall Street Journal* in 1989. "Band-Aids won't work anymore. We need a total restructuring."

Dangers of Denial

Like the argument that there's no more room in America for immigrants, the argument that the American economy can utilize only highly skilled and highly educated immigrants simply doesn't hold up under scrutiny. America will suffer badly if it fails to acknowledge that it cannot merely import some specialized forms of workplace expertise through immigration while prohibiting mass immigration—and that it must make the investment in overall work force development that the new world of work requires.

The American society for Training and Development

made these dangers very clear in a report it issued in 1989 called *The Learning Enterprise.*

"When the baby boom moved into the workplace, it found too few good jobs and promotions to go around. But the generations that will follow will be small in comparison with the baby boom," the report said. "Unfortunately, the sense that people are oversupplied may mislead Americans into a strategy that favors investment in machines, financial capital and extracted resources over investments in the education and training of people. In a very short time, however, such a curse of action would prove a serious economic error."

Despite all this evidence that education and training are the keys to the success of *all* of America's work force, no matter where they were born, many Americans continue to resent and even protest the education of new immigrants.

In Raymondville, Texas, for example, there is a special home and school called the International Emergency Shelter for youngsters less than seventeen years old who cross the Rio Grande into America without their parents. They are not old enough to be deported under American law, and their parents usually have learned about that loophole through the grapevine of poverty.

Wanting their children to have a chance at a decent life, parents from Mexico and Central America often give their kids what little cash they have, kiss them goodbye, then send them running and swimming for the border of the United States. Swim to America, they say, and maybe someday you'll be able to help us all; but, at the very least, you won't grind your life away here in the mud or die as a soldier of a corrupt dictator.

Many of those young people are captured by the U.S.

Border Patrol and taken to the International Emergency Shelter and similar facilities run by charitable groups. There they are taught to speak English and become familiar with the customs of America. They are taught how to fill out a job application properly and the smart way to rent a place to live—things that, as personnel executives know all too well, a depressingly large percentage of America's native-born work force doesn't know how to do.

Yet there is protest. Neighbors of such facilities often call to complain, an administrator of one of them told *The New York Times* in 1989. When the shelter she manages was under construction, she said, "We got calls from people who wanted to know why we were building swimming pools for illegal aliens."

CHAPTER 9

People, Politics and the Future of Immigration

PEOPLE'S ATTITUDES AND, consequently, the course of politics change much more slowly than is usually hoped or assumed. The fast pace of the day-to-day news reports makes it appear that the course of citizen sentiment changes rapidly in America. But in reality the process is an extremely slow one—particularly when the issues involve the tensions between America's varied immigrant groups.

For example, my first up-close encounter with the potentially violent emotions generated by America's immigrant rivalries occurred back in the fall of 1968. I was 18 years old and lying on a muddy rifle range at Fort Leonard Wood, Missouri. The Vietnam war was in full swing. I and my peers from America's white lower-working class, along with the young men of the black and Hispanic ghettos, were being taught how to kill in anticipation of a free trip—often one way—to Southeast Asia.

Such rifle ranges were at that time equipped with rows of plastic targets, shaped like the upper half of a human being, that were attached to hinge-like electrical devices that could make them stand up, one-by-one at random, when the range operator threw the appropriate switch. As trainee soldiers, our assignment was to scan the horizon and shoot at any target that popped up in our line of fire. If a bullet hit the target, the bullet passed through and eventually buried itself in a dirt bank, but the vibration caused by its passing triggered a device that made the target go down, letting us know that we had been successful in killing our imaginary enemy.

Our trainers in other forms of killing had conjured up an inspiration for their students images of an enemy named "Charley," an abbreviated form of "Charley Cong," which was then a popular corruption of "Viet Cong." "Get Charley!" they'd scream as we shoved bayonets into the torsos of rag-skinned dummies, or lobbed hand grenades at obsolete trucks and tanks. But on our first morning on the rifle range, the black drill sergeant who was running it from a tower equipped with a public-address system had a different enemy in mind.

"There he is, it's Mayor Daley," the sergeant boomed through the loudspeaker as targets began popping up at the far end of the range. "Get him!" he commanded, and the loud cracks of rifle fire quickly filled the air.

Being a white kid from the coal fields of Pennsylvania, I really wasn't sure who Mayor Daley was, or why I should want to shoot at him. But having targets left standing at the end of such an exercise was not something a young soldier wanted to do. So I lay there nonchalantly, beneath clouds of powder smoke that made the scene seem surreal, leaning against a pile of sandbags and pumping clip after clip of bullets from by semiautomatic rifle into Mayor Daley in effigy. For several hours the mayor kept popping up, and I kept shooting him down at the urgings of our black instructor.

That wasn't the last time I shot Mayor Daley. We spent about two weeks on that range, shooting at Mayor Daley whenever and wherever he popped up. Eventually, I even got a little medal for shooting Mayor Daley down an above-average number of times. By the end of that training period, and after such behavior reinforcement, it seemed only natural that Mayor Daley was someone you should want to shoot at.

Virtually all our black rifle-range instructors liked to think of Mayor Daley as an appropriate target for hostile action by the U.S. Army, it seemed, and they succeeded in imbuing us with similar sentiments. I even wondered at times whether the boys who were really fighting over in Southeast Asia would say to themselves as their bullet passed through the chest of a Vietnamese opponent, "Gotcha, Mayor Daley!"

It wasn't until a few years later, however, that I began to understand the hostility of those drill sergeants toward the man called "Mayor Daley." I never had to go to Vietnam because, despite my lack of the kind of political or business connections that kept most baby boomers form the middle class and above safely stored on college campuses in those years when their poorer counterparts were trading bullets with "Charley," I managed to get myself assigned to a reserve military police unit stateside and, later, to the Criminal Investigation Department Command, the Army's version of the Federal Bureau of Investigation.

Criminal investigators are schooled in human nature, among other things, so I soon learned a lot about the psychology of military life. Eventually I came to understand that most of those black rifle-range instructors had been Army career men, "lifers" for whom Chicago was home. Fort Leonard Wood was a basic training facility relatively close to Chicago, so that's where they liked to be stationed. And in Chicago the name of Mayor Richard J. Daley was virtually synonymous with hatred, fear and intimidation of blacks.

After managing to stay alive during their thankless 13 months in Vietnam, those black drill sergeants had had to come home and watch their families do war with the Daley-controlled Chicago police department. Luckily for Mayor Daley and the rest of white Chicago, those battle-hardened drill sergeants had been professional enough to vent their rage on the rifle range.

During the ensuing two decades I nearly forgot about the rifle range and Mayor Daley. But in 1989 it suddenly seemed as though he had recovered from those tens of thousands of bullet wounds inflicted on him at Fort Leonard Wood. Once again the headlines were talking about Chicago having a "Mayor Daley" and I could almost smell the powder smoke.

This time, however, it was his son, Richard M. Daley. But, other than the generational transition, things hadn't changed much in 20 years. The incumbent mayor was Eugene Sawyer, a black, and most black voters were supporting him. Daley was getting most of the white votes. The contest was summed up by a simple headline in The New York Times: "Race Overrides All in the Chicago Vote".

America was no longer at war, of course, so the throngs of boot soldiers and their ghetto-bred trainers were no longer residing at Fort Leonard Wood. But I'm sure that if they had been, they'd still be shooting at a "Mayor Daley."

Cultural Revenge

The continuing political success of the Daleys and their ilk demonstrates the slowness with which the scars of America's immigrant rivalries heal. But those rivalries have, in some cases, had a positive, constructive effect on American politics. Inner rage can be converted into impassioned leadership. The humanistic, egalitarian tendencies of Boston's Mayor Ray Flynn, for example, have been attributed by many to his humiliating experiences as the grandson of Irish immigrants.

Although many Irish-American families such as the Kennedys rose to fame and wealth in Boston, many more have remained in the blue-collar ranks. Indeed, because of its large Irish-American working class that never really rose above its immigrant role as imported labor, Boston is one of the few American cities left where a fair number of cab drivers speak English.

Mayor Flynn's father, a longshoreman, developed tuberculosis while only in his forties. His family lived in working-class South Boston and was on welfare for a time after the elder Mr. Flynn became ill. Eventually, the future mayor's mother got a job downtown as a cleaning lady.

"He's just an Irish-Catholic kid from the wrong side of the tracks," said one of his advisors, who chose to remain anonymous, in a 1989 interview with *The Boston Globe*. "There's a tremendous desire to succeed and to overcome doubters. To call it ambition is not to do it justice, because what it really is is revenge. Cultural revenge. . . ."

How has Flynn's craving for cultural revenge manifested itself? Don Muhammad, a minister with the Nation of Islam in Boston's lower-class Roxbury section and a prominent black leader there, told The Globe that Flynn "is genuinely concerned about the smallest of details" that affect human lives. "Most big-city mayors don't deal with the grass-roots problems that Ray Flynn deals with," he added.

Prior to his administration, the city had decided to close Boston City Hospital, where Mayor Flynn had been born. But when he visited the hospital after becoming mayor, he saw more clearly that it served many of Boston's poorest people. Flynn resolved to make it a personal goal to rebuild the hospital better than ever before.

"If I have my way, we'll have the best-quality health care facility in America," he said. "And it won't make any difference whether you're John Rockefeller walking in the door or some cleaning woman from South Boston."

Obviously, Flynn's style of leadership is not one that is emotionally detached. And the emotions that move him obviously date back several decades. But certainly the emotions that motivate him are far more admirable and desirable than those that have given us the Mayors Daley. Although the wounds of immigrant rivalry heal slowly, they don't always leave ugly scars.

The Power of 'Old Money'

Given this slow rate of healing, and the diversity and complexity of the emotions that have been generated by America's long tradition of immigrant rivalries, what chance is there of America assimilating all the newcomers it needs in a manner, and on a schedule, that will prevent at least some of the economic problems that are destined to arise from America's continuing tradition of clashing racial and ethnic values?

The necessary leadership is not likely to come from the top of America's socioeconomic structure. In fact, despite the growing influence of America's diverse races and cultures at the lower levels of government, the roots of America's highest levels of political power continue to be planted firmly in the economic soil claimed by some of the country's earliest arrivals from the British Empire.

For example, while covering government as a newspaper reporter in the late 1970s, I was introduced to a very affable young man in the requisite navy blue Brooks Brothers suit and horn-rimmed glasses who was then governor of West Virginia. It was very important to meet him, said the excited political functionaries who buzzed around him, because he was a sure bet to be the president of the United States some day.

He name was John Davison Rockefeller IV, but as we shook hands he told me to call him just "Jay." Except for the high recognition value of his surname, he was a virtual unknown outside West Virginia. He wasn't a native son of West Virginia, and he hadn't done anything particularly noteworthy with his life that would make him stand above the rest of us. His family tree could be traced back to some of the earliest Scottish immigrants to America, however, and his great-grandfather had acquired enormous wealth through the illegal monopolization of America's petroleum supplies during the early decades of the country's mechanization when most Americans' forebears were just arriving.

Most importantly, Jay was the Rockefeller designated to take control of American government, so his famous and wealthy family had dumped money on the impoverished state of West Virginia until Jay was firmly ensconced in the governor's mansion—and, consequently, on his way to Washington.

In the more than ten years that have passed since that introduction, I've often told friends about my encounter with Jay and about the fact that the Rockefellers had resolved to buy the presidency for him. But most people harbor more awe and less cynicism than journalists; consequently, they don't believe that one of the most powerful elective offices on earth is there for the plucking by anyone with enough money. In particular, they reject the idea that America has a defacto ruling class that is still made up of primarily Anglo Saxon genes. My report on Jay Rockefeller has, needless to say, been scoffed at many times.

As America heads for the end of the 20th century, however, my prediction is gaining credibility. Jay has moved up to being a U.S. Senator from West Virginia and now lives in a different mansion, this one in Washington, D.C. It's known as "The Rocks," and even jaded Washingtonians gasped in February 1989 when he refinanced it and the news broke that Jay pays on a mortgage of $15.8 million. Obviously, he has the money it takes to stay in Washington for a long, long time.

At this writing, Jay still hadn't done anything particularly noteworthy. But the world can expect to see him do so as the 21st century approaches. Like most of his contemporaries in the Senate, he has maintained what the American news media have come to refer as "Kennedyesque" look and style necessary to win babyboomer votes. At some point, Jay will begin chairing controversial committee investigations and proposing controversial legislation, making headlines for the newspapers and soundbytes for the television cameras.

Because his political foundation is made up of family money and the power it can buy, not spontaneous voter approval, he won't be inhibited by the pragmatic home-state concerns that temper most politicians. Like Geraldo Rivera, Jay will begin benefitting from the fact that many hype-sodden Americans can no longer differentiate between admiration and mere name recognition.

The ability of "old money" such as that which supports Jay, to buy the presidency was confirmed anew in 1989 when America installed as its president another affable-but-mundane multimillionaire who can trace his bloodlines to the British royal family—and who was once quoted by *The Wall Street Journal* as saying that he believes in the concept of *noblesse oblige,* the responsibility of the noble-born to rule.

By President Bush's side at that inauguration was Dan Quayle, the bumbling son of a wealthy old Anglo-Saxon family whose grandfather, Eugene Pulliam, was a leading supporter of Senator McCarthy's communist witchhunts of the '50s—and whose father was a member of the ultra-racist and anti-immigration John Birch Society.

So with just a little more time, a little more media exposure and the expenditure of just a few more millions of his family's dollars, Senator Rockefeller might become a household name. Then, like game-show numbers-turner Vanna White, he'll be able to command the knee-jerk approval of millions of American voters and begin planning the short-but-profound move from The Rocks to The White House. America's Anglo-Saxon circle of power will not have been broken.

"President Rockefeller" would be unlikely, of course, to experience the empathy for those experiencing the immigrant syndrome in contemporary America in the way that Boston's Mayor Flynn does. The royally reared President Rockefeller would have no need for cultural revenge. So if, as Woody Guthrie often argued, only those who have personally experienced hard times are qualified to sing about them, President Rockefeller would not be able to make the kind of music that will be necessary to lead the world's racial and ethnic melting pot successfully and peacefully into the 21st century.

Shifting Tides

But what if people like the Bushes, the Quayles and the Rockefellers have calculated incorrectly? What if there is a new era of economic awareness, understanding and activism afoot in America? What if the popularity of singer-songwriter Tracy Chapman's ghetto laments and her whispered intimations of an impending black revolution portend a renewal of the egalitarian and humanistic sentiments and crusades that flavored the '60s until Vietnam became America's political preoccupation?

Will the need of tens of millions of Americans for cultural revenge manifest itself by allowing the country to accept, or even welcome, the masses of immigrants it needs to succeed in the global economy of the 21st century? Is it possible that the face in America's mirror has already changed more than the old Anglo-Saxon guard realizes, making the suffering and death inflicted on Hispanics and Asians along America's borders and shores less and less tolerable?

Can the restraints imposed on the American economy by jobilism ever be overcome? Will America ever be able to consider the issue of immigration scientifically instead of emotionally, allowing prosperity to follow where immigrants go?

One of the people most qualified to respond to such questions is Bill Boyarsky, city-county editor of the *Los Angeles Times*, and president (at this writing) of the Los Angeles Chapter of the Society of Professional Journalists. Indeed, in 1989 Boyarsky found himself in the national news as an innocent participant in a public scandal involving ethnic rivalries and the management of the *Los Angeles Times*.

The *Times* had long supported Tom Bradley as mayor of Los Angeles because, according to most expert observers, Bradley was black and that fact helped to keep a lid on the racial and ethnic tensions inherent to contemporary Los Angeles. In early 1989, a reporter for the *Los Angeles Times* had written a story that detailed what appeared to be a corrupt relationship between Mayor Bradley and a financial institution. Boyarsky edited and approved that story for publication, but its publication was stopped by the newspaper's managing editor.

A few months later the competing *Los Angeles Herald Examiner* broke a similar story. Other national news media soon began reporting on the situation, and the top management of the *Los Angeles Times* was embarrassed into abandoning its attempts at engineering racial and ethnic harmony—and into publishing the truth about Bradley that Boyarsky had wanted to publish all along.

In addition to holding that position as a principal gatekeeper for news in America's immigration capital of the '90s, Boyarsky is a veteran correspondent from the front lines of America's immigrant rivalries. He was a political writer for the Associated Press for about a decade before joining the *Los Angeles Times* in 1970 to handle similar categories of news.

"In Los Angeles, if you're covering local politics, you're covering a lot of black and Hispanic politics, and Jewish politics—you're covering ethnic politics," Boyarsky pointed out in a conversation we had just a few weeks before the Bradley scandal broke. Working within the realm of ethnic politics he has learned significant lessons about the power of America's immigrant rivalries.

In particular, Boyarsky—whose grandparents were Jews who came to America from Russia early in the 20th century—recalls an assignment he shared with a black female reporter in the mid 1980s: Louis Farrakhan, the Black Muslim leader who has been quoted as calling Adolph Hitler "a great man" and describing Judaism as a "gutter religion," was scheduled to deliver a major address in Los Angeles.

"The question was Mayor Bradley's role—should he denounce him (Farrakhan) as the Jews wanted or should be not denounce him—it was a hell of a flap," Boyarsky said. "The reporter who covered it with me was a black, Janet Clayton. She covered the blacks, and I covered the Jews, basically.

"In the evening we would talk about this thing a lot because it was a very consuming story. And it was interesting working together, a black and a Jew; she was younger and I was older; a man working with a woman—there were all these very interesting combinations.

"She said that the reason that it was such a big issue was that it dealt with the greatest insecurity of those peoples: First, the Jews were telling the black leaders, who were black males, that they wanted them to do something. It dealt with the greatest insecurity of black males, that of not really having any power," he said.

"With the Jews, she said, it dealt with their deepest insecurity, which is anti-semitism, the holocaust. That's what I call quite a brilliant ethnic insight.

"I said 'Janet, when this guy talks, I see ovens. If this guy were ever in charge, he'd been pulling me to the ovens, that's how I feel about it.' She could see how I felt about it. There were two people, and each had personal ethnic insights," he said.

Such diversity of viewpoints among America's immigrant groups will never dissipate to the point where immigration will become a smooth process, Boyarsky predicts, even though contemporary immigrant groups will eventually be assimilated into the American economy just as earlier immigrant waves were.

"It will be very painful, accompanied by a lot of prejudice—ethnic groups never get along well in America; never have, never will," he says. As evidence, he points to organizations representing second- and third-generation Mexican-Americans that favor deportation of undocumented Mexican workers and the institution of English-only laws.

Although the rivalries will continue to dominate immigration policy, not all the effect of immigrant rivalries will be bad, he says. "It's a long, painful process. We're used to that in America. That's how we were created, and that gives us a lot of strength."

Black Ambivalence

Hispanic and Asian organizations have dominated contemporary public debate of America's immigration policies in the latter part of the 20th century, of course, and the consensus among them is overwhelmingly in favor of continuing and expanding the politically potent concept of family reunification.

Meanwhile, most native-born white Americans of European descent are not outwardly organized around immigration issues. But history proves that their fears of mass immigration are made known and served through more subtle channels and mechanisms; the political trend toward restricting immigration to well-educated and highly skilled persons is evidence of that.

However, of all the racial and ethnic groups in America, native-born blacks logically should comprise the group most concerned and vocal about immigration trends. Dr. Robert B. Hill, director of the Urban Research Center at Morgan State University in Maryland and former research director of the Urban League, points out, for example, that because unpaid slavery and subsequent barriers delayed the participation of African-Americans in the American economy, very few native-born blacks have ever accrued the level of net worth required for permanent membership in America's middle class. Consequently, native-born black Americans are most vulnerable to economic mood swings.

During the mass immigrations of whites from Europe in the early 20th century, Hill notes, native-born black Americans were very aware of the fact that industrial employers in the North generally preferred white immigrants from Europe to blacks migrating from the South. The concerns and frustrations of the blacks weren't given voice in the American news media of those times, but they were frequently expressed around the dinner table in black homes. During that period in the history of American immigration, Hill says, native-born blacks "got shafted."

Despite those experiences, however, ambivalence dominates the contemporary viewpoint of the native-born black community toward immigration issues. Some of this is due, of course, to the relationship between native-born blacks and newly arrived immigrant groups that Thomas Muller's research has demonstrated: The arrival of new immigrant groups has, in many cases, allowed native-born blacks to rise higher into the socioeconomic structures.

Hill points out, however, that the apparent ambivalence also stems from the fact that the ethnic roots of America's black community are not as uniform as commonly depicted by the news media and, consequently, perceived by the typical white citizen. Many contemporary immigrants classified as "black," for example, are also Hispanics—many of them descendants of African-born slaves imported to or abandoned in Spanish-speaking countries in the 19th century, whose family cultures and traditions evolved differently than that of the blacks enslaved in America.

The situation is further confused by the fact that some people who are not categorized as "black" in their native lands are given that designation by immigration and census officials in the United States. "More and more of them are having to go through this very interesting process," Hill says, "because if they look black, they are treated as black. So more and more immigrants are resonating to black communities and relationships and this is enhancing the numbers of immigrants in the black community.

"Although some other countries such as Brazil have a mixture group, we refuse to have it. We have a dichotomous system here: If you've got any black blood, no matter what you look like, you're black. I find it very interesting that we can't find that middle niche here."

Many of the blacks who immigrated to America from such countries as the Dominican Republic prior to the legislation of the family reunification concept in the mid '60s, for example, were allowed into America on the basis of education and job skills. Now they want very much to bring their families to America without consideration of education or job skills, every bit as much as Asian and other Hispanic immigrants do.

"There is a bias in the issue of immigration as it relates to blacks in that it is typically discussed only in the negative sense of immigrants taking away jobs," Hill says, but in reality there are more complex issues involved. For example, black Haitians who immigrated to America in the 1980s were not given the welcome by the government that non-black Cubans received in earlier decades, and some Southeast Asians who immigrated to America after the Vietnam War were supported by the U.S. government in ways that equally impoverished American-born blacks were not.

Nevertheless, the decline in the economic prospects for America's middle class is likely to hit paycheck-class blacks harder or more quickly than their white counterparts, Hill believes, so resistance to mass immigration may develop among native-born black Americans. "Whenever America has had hard times, we want to get rid of immigrants. Whenever we've had boom times and we could exploit them, we've imported them. That has really been the nature of America's immigration policy," Hill points out.

Jewish Empathy

One group that will undoubtedly serve as a major influence on the formation of future immigration policy is America's Jewish community. Because of their cultural emphasis on intellectualism and their economic successes in America in recent decades, America's Jews can never be ignored by politicians at any level.

One of the people who best understands the position of America's Jewish community on the subject of immigration is Deborah E. Lipstadt, an assistant professor of Jewish history at Occidental College in Los Angeles and author of *Beyond Belief* (The Free Press, 1986), a brilliant study of the American news media's failure to acknowledge the horrors of the Nazi holocaust until Hitler's forces were well along in their campaign against the Jews.

America's tradition of blaming a wide variety of problems on immigrants and would-be immigrants has long plagued Jews, she points out. It reached a particularly absurd level in the 1930s, when some American writers and commentators began to argue that to allow Europe's tormented Jews to enter America would be detrimental because it would *cause* anti-semitism in America. Other American writers of those times argued that the political and military turmoil in Europe was being caused by an excess of people there, and they used that as an argument against allowing many of those uprooted by the Nazis to enter America.

"They blamed the victims," she notes. "The victims got the blame for what was going on."

Lipstadt acknowledges that she has experienced personally the gut resentment that most Americans feel when a neighborhood near them begins to fill up with impoverished, newly arrived immigrants. She uses her mother's situation as a condominium dweller in South Florida as an example: Hordes of young, impoverished immigrants from Latin America are filling in every vacant space between the homes and apartments of American-born retirees who migrated from the Northeast to Florida in hope of finding room for relaxation. Consequently, to her, her mother and her mother's American-born neighbors, immigration is something that on its surface appears to be something that needs to be stopped.

But that type of emotion seems often to be counterbalanced by the still-fresh memories of human strife that exist in the minds of many Jewish-Americans. Campaigns conducted by American Jewish leaders in the 1980s to win additional immigration slots for Russian Jews, for example, were not self-centered.

"They got very upset when added slots were given to Russian Jews at the expense of Southeast Asians," Lipstadt points out. "The Jews say, 'It shouldn't be either—or.'" To survive the Nazi holocaust, she says, many Jewish-Americans had to have "luck, luck, luck, and luck tens times over," only to find that other countries had closed the door to them after they had managed to escape the terror.

"I think we'll come down on the side of keeping the door open, because we cannot say 'Close it to everyone but Jews.' For many Jews, the immigration experience is still too close for that—the immigration experience occurred only a generation or two ago," she says.

Japanese Component

There is one thing that is certain about the importance of immigration issues in American politics and economics: It won't diminish for many decades to come. As *Time* magazine pointed out in 1989: "The beacon of hope for a better life in America burns brightest for those who endure the most profound debasement in their native land. While the U.S. today is ill-equipped to take them all in, the dream lives on. For that reason, the immigration wave is not likely to slow."

What's more, America is far from being alone in its quandary over immigration policies. Europe has in recent years been experiencing relatively small political skirmishes over immigration. And now that Japan has been able to claim the leadership role in global economics—partly because Americans have spent much of their economic energy in recent years on the pursuit of jobilism—Japan is also developing a need for ever-increasing supplies of labor.

In the late 1980s, however, Japan began to experience a rash of clashes between the ever-changing nature of capitalism, the "creative destruction" that noted American economist Joseph Schumpeter described decades ago, and the strong cultural craving of the Japanese people for unchanging tradition and rigid social hierarchies. "But soon a new question may become an even starker symbol of the pull between capitalism and Japanese-ness," noted *Business Month* magazine in March 1989, "whether Japan can afford economically to keep foreign laborers out—or to afford culturally to let them in.

"If this were a purely economic decision, it would be simple to make: Japan's businesses need more labor, particularly unskilled labor, than Japanese society is now supplying . . . in general, Japan is straining against the limits of full employment."

It is very likely that a day will come when American and Japanese companies find themselves competing for unskilled labor from less developed countries. But a twist that most Americans have never anticipated may occur: Japanese companies may decide that they would prefer to have those immigrant workers on the payrolls of the many factories they have built and are building in America.

There are many indications—such as the fact that the Japanese have begun buying small American colleges and using them to familiarize their managers of the future with the American culture, as well as the energy with which the Japanese business community has moved into the border *maquiladoras*—that the Japanese have decided to solve their conflict between the need for additional labor and their culture resistance to immigrants by simply employing non-Japanese workers somewhere other than in Japan.

America and Mexico may eventually become, as the state of Tennessee already has, a sort of manufacturing colony in relation to the Japanese economy. If that comes to pass, of course, the tensions surrounding immigration to America will enter an even higher level of fervor and complexity. The Japanese have already exhibited their ability to use jobilism to sway American political decisions: They have, for example, persuaded the United States government to pay them to train Americans to work in their American-based auto plants. There's no reason to think that Japanese industrialists won't use the power of jobilism even more forcefully should their need for labor begin to conflict with America's resistance to immigrants.

"Just One Lifeboat"

For these and many other reasons, America's difficulties with the subject of immigration will continue at one level or another for many decades to come. Evidence to the contrary notwithstanding, America is likely to continue to search for reasons to resist the arrival of new waves of workers. However, there is one very large thought I've encountered that seems to transcend all the point-by-point disputes over immigration, that seems to have the potential to reduce them all to pettiness.

The thought comes from the mind of Alan Lomax, who has dedicated his life to recording and analyzing the music and dance of cultures around the world, but particularly those in America. Standing back from the rivalries among various cultures, he attributes the very survival of mankind to the diversity of cultures existing among all the peoples of the world.

"Man's biggest contribution on the planet is the invention of a multitude of cultures, each suited to a certain time and environment," Lomax once told *The New York Times*. "Each culture's complex of artistic patterns sums up the healthy modes of survival. We have to think into the future how to maintain all the potential that the human spirit has spun out in the last 90,000 years.

"To have only one culture would be like facing the Atlantic with a storm on the way—and with just one lifeboat."

Index

Greenleaf, Barbara Kaye, 59–60, 61
Greenspan, Hank, 102, 109
Guthrie, Woody, 82–85, 86, 98, 101, 111, 242; "This Land Is Your Land," 82, 84–85

Hale, David, 228–230
Hill, Robert B., 246–248
Hitler, Adolph, 73–74, 244

immigrants, African, 57–59; and America's changing face, 46–52, 179–180; and employment of native blacks, 245–248; and "Ethnic Pop," 45–46; and global job market, 251–252; and Jews, 249–250; and jobilism, 41–43; and manual labor, 222–225; and prosperity, 44–45, 171–203; and Refugee Act of 1953, 116–117; and "twin factory" system, 23–24, 25, 43–44; anti-, sentiments, 39, 40–41, 61–63, 65, 69, 74–75, 77–79, 117, 126–128, 146, 169, 176, 231; Asian, 48, 49, 62–63, 71, 76, 183, 199; atrocities of illegal, 38–39; central economic planning and, 191–196; Chinese, 27–28, 63, 182; credentialling of, 150–151, 168; Cuban, 117; cultural revenge, 237–238; "Dillingham Commission" report on, 70–71; discrimination against, 39, 61–63, 65–67, 71, 79, 118, 124, 129; education and training of, 219–232; effects of, on U.S. economy, 28–31, 44–45, 171–203; European, 56–57, 67–68, 73, 77, 78, 246; Filipino, 27; French Canadian, 61–62; from communist countries, 78; German, 61–62, 63, 69; German Jewish, 74–75; illegal, 26–28, 30–31, 128, 178–179, 185–186, 231–232; Industrial Revolution, 53–66, 93; intermarriage, 47–49; internal, 75–76, 247–248; Irish, 59–62, 63, 182; Italian, 68–69, 70; living space and location for, 204–218; Nicaraguan, 79–80; 1989 number of, 38; racist killings of, 39; restric-

tions on, 27–28, 73–76, 114–115, 127–130, 136, 181–186; rivalries, 53–80, 120, 168, 233–253; self-perpetuating poverty and, 64–67; "triangle of confusion" and, 28–31; versus the paycheck, 139–169
immigration, and employment 128–130, 133, 136–138, 174–181, 251–252; and investment in America, 135; and jobilism, 41–43, 84, 130, 131, 135; dangers of restriction, 181–186; during WWII, 76–77; effects of, on ethnic minorities, 184–186; European 198–199; formula for expansion, 186–189; policies, 37–38, 40–41, 69–71, 73, 106–107, 181, 245–253; restrictions, 27–28, 73–76, 114–115, 127–130, 136, 181–186; "system" of family units, 125–126
Immigration Act of 1989, 133, 135, 174
Immigration and Nationality Act of 1965, 122–123, 126, 127
Immigration and Naturalization Service (INS), 39, 110, 190–191; Guide to Immigration Benefits, 190; policy regulations, 114–115
immigration policies, 37–38, 40–41, 69–71, 73, 106–107, 181, 245–253; and danger of restricting immigrants, 181–186; and "Dillingham Commission," 70–71; and INS, 39, 114–115; and political refugees, 127–128; and the Red Scare, 87; communism and, 100, 106–107, 110–111, 115, 136; contemporary, 114–138; employment and, 128–130, 133, 136–138, 174–203; family reunification and, 116–120, 122, 123, 124, 126, 133; in 1800s, 62–63, 67–68; in 1900s, 69–70; job skills and, 124–125, 128, 133, 136–138; LeMay on, 129–130; McCarran and, 99–100, 102–103, 104–106, 108; 1980s; 131–135; post-WWII, 77, 78, 88, 91, 99; reforms of JFK, 117–118, 119, 121
Ives, Burl, 84, 97–98, 101